W9-BCB-127

*A
Harlequin
Romance*

OTHER

Harlequin Romances

by DORIS E. SMITH

1341—FIRE IS FOR SHARING
1427—TO SING ME HOME
1454—SEVEN OF MAGPIES
1599—DEAR DECEIVER
1690—THE ONE AND ONLY
1922—COTSWOLD HONEY

COTSWOLD HONEY

by

DORIS E. SMITH

HARLEQUIN BOOKS   TORONTO
WINNIPEG

Harlequin edition published November 1975

SBN 373-01922-X

Original hard cover edition published in 1975
by Mills & Boon Limited.

Printed in Canada

1922

CHAPTER ONE

WITH Eve it was an apple, with Charlotte Lavender a fox. She was four years, fifty-one weeks and six days old and the fox was stuffed and in a glass case in the window of an antique shop. Charlotte, a rosy dumpling, was trotting along by the side of her grandmother who had decided she was a sensible child and capable of choosing her fifth birthday present.

When Charlotte saw the fox she said immediately : "I'd like that," and, for her grandmother, the fair flowers of paradise began to wither.

"She doesn't get that from Ivor," she thought fearfully. "It's Ruth." Ivor Lavender, her son and Charlotte's father, had died six months before. Ruth, her daughter-in-law, was American and had run after Ivor—all the way from Pennsylvania. "She would approve of the fox," Charlotte's grandmother thought, hustling Charlotte away from the window. "That's Ruth all over. Bizarre."

The fox constituted the first irrational moment in Charlotte's life and in the nicest possible way she had never been allowed to forget it.

"When I think what a silly little girl you were, Charlie," her grandmother was fond of saying, "I'm so thankful for the way you grew up. So like your father. So logical."

She died when Charlotte was seventeen. They had been close friends and she was deeply mourned. She had also done her work extremely well.

Too well? Ruth Lavender sometimes wondered, but she too had respected and cared for the old lady. Mary Lavender had been kind and generous, she had given Charlie ballast. Is it really possible, Ruth had often asked herself, that I have a baby who never gets fussed, never makes a mistake, never gets in hot water, never loses her head?

She herself had spent forty-nine enjoyable years consistently doing all four and at the end of them she was a

5

popular member of staff on a magazine. Charlotte, now twenty-one, was a veterinary nurse and worked in an animal hospital also in London.

On normal duty her day began at nine after a journey by train and underground that could take the best part of an hour. Ruth had more time but additional mileage, so they had brought breakfast to a fine art.

This morning Charlotte's dark blonde head popped briskly into the kitchen to the not unfamiliar sight of her mother perched on a stool at the bar, in front of her a glass of orange juice and the newspaper, behind her the cooker and thin blue smoke trails.

"Mummy! The toast!"

Ivor Lavender had discovered twenty-five years ago that there was no use being angry. Charlotte, throwing out the 'burnt offering', shook her head affectionately at the culprit.

It was then she saw the letter propped against the second glass of orange juice. It was addressed 'Miss C. Lavender' in a flowing hand and when she picked it up the postmark, as expected, was Gloucestershire. She looked thoughtfully at her mother's fair hair and smoked glasses. There was no need to feel guilty. She knew she was free to set up on her own if ever she so desired. Ruth Lavender was not the lonely type.

"I can take it or leave it," Charlotte thought, putting the letter into her handbag.

At few other moments had her dearly loved grandmother seemed so near. "She would think I was running away; she would say : 'Dear child, what has happened to your backbone?'" Charlotte thought, peering at the reflection of her eyebrows as she brushed them. They were dark brows cutting across a little rosy face. Short hair, the colour of strained honey, feathered into her neck. Her nose turned up. It was very nearly the same face that had looked away from the stuffed fox and up into her grandmother's. Charlotte had not changed much. She still thought it was dreadful to make a mistake. "I'm not making one now, Don. Am I?" she questioned silently.

Don was a vet at the hospital. Their first person-to-person contact had been an after-hours emergency. A

6

motorist had knocked down and injured a terrier which had streaked off the pavement under his front wheel. Visibly shaken, he had turned up at the clinic with the casualty and the tearful eight-year-old owner. It had been Charlotte's week for late duty and she had assisted in the theatre. Don had not been long on the staff of the hospital and he was anxious. Charlie had been in there with him, anticipating his every move. The little dog had survived.

Charlie knew now exactly why Don had wanted her company that evening when they went off duty. It had been a chemical reaction, not a miracle. The steak house to which he had brought her had been warm and full of nice clatter and succulent aromas. They were late and healthily hungry and they had won a battle. He had stretched across the table and taken her hand. "You're lovely," he had said. After that they had started going out together.

It was Don's first job in London, he had studied in Bristol and worked for a year in Wiltshire. He was ambitious and talked of going abroad. In the early stages Charlie had been clear-sighted. Don had a long way to go before thinking of settling down. His looks would bring him not just a girl but a fan club in every port. But as the weeks went by her memory grew bad. She forgot the sense and let herself think 'we' instead of 'I'.

The first cloud was not even as big as a man's hand. He was invited to lunch one Sunday, but at the eleventh hour he had gone down with 'flu and Charlie, deeply disappointed, had never been quite sure that he was not secretly relieved. Somehow she had got cold feet about renewing the invitation, and anyway her mother had been bringing work home every weekend. Silly as it seemed, Mummy, the most casual and successful person about relationships, would never know without having it spelled out how urgent and how terrifying a simple lunch date could be.

Charlie was sorry now that the meeting had never materialised. Win or lose, they would have liked each other. Mummy was such a marvellous person, full of fun, continually sending herself up. Charlie knew that given a million years she could never be like that. She was a quiet one; there were jobs to be done and she got on with them.

Once from the passage that housed the sterilisers she had heard two of the junior vets talking about her. "I know she's a doll to look at," one of them had said. "But she's not switched on."

'Not switched on'—and now not brave enough to stay around and see Don turning to someone else. The new girl in the research unit was not pretty, but she had a certain way of looking and moving that caught the eye. She was exceedingly good at her job and, outside it, exceedingly arrogant. She had stood Don up one night. Charlie was not supposed to know this, but at coffee break next day someone had let the cat out of the bag. The entire common room had frozen into silence and well-meaning friends had tried to cover up. It had been horrible.

Charlie might not have been the life and soul of the party, but she had always been for people. Hers was the ear to which the other nurses came when there was illness or other trouble at home. It was a measure of her state of mind that suddenly she found herself wishing they wouldn't. All she wanted was to be left alone. For days on end she tried to avoid the common room. As soon as she came off duty she scuttled out of the building. When Don was around she never knew whether to be unobtrusive or to laugh a lot. It really didn't matter since each was a ghastly flop.

The climax came when Mr. Lemon, the most senior vet at the hospital, had to reprimand her for not having the right number of sutures mounted and to her horror her eyes started to fill.

Was it coincidence that two days later he had walked into the X-ray department where she was calming a nervous patient before laying it under the machine. The patient, a Labrador, had been injected with a sedative, she was already quietening down and Charlie was gentling her neck. It had been a surprise to look up and see Mr. Lemon, still more so when he had started chatting to her about a visit he had made the previous day to an affiliated animal rest centre in South Gloucestershire. En route he had passed through Hopehampton and had looked up the local vet, Kenneth Carr. He had found him in some confusion having just lost the nurse/secretary who had been

8

with him for years.

"As a matter of fact he asked if I knew anyone who might replace her. I told him it wasn't likely but I'd put the word round."

Charlie's patient by then had been quite relaxed. As she laid her gently in position Mr. Lemon had started to move away. Perhaps that had decided her. Who knew when such a solution would present itself again?

"Mr. Lemon," she had said jerkily. "Before you go. I might be interested myself."

The letter, read in the train, was a pleasure to the eye. The rolling open handwriting that had graced the envelope looked even better with margins and paragraphs. Momentarily, the Piccadilly Line, in the morning rush hour, faded and Charlie's thoughts turned yet again to her grandmother. Mary Lavender had been particular about good writing. In fact, this letter linked easily with the blue-ribboned pile that they had found and burned after her death.

But of course, that was nonsense because those had been love letters. This communication was strictly business.

Dear Miss Lavender,

Adverting to your letter and the commendation from my friend Tom Lemon, I am interested in your application, although I feel you would find this practice in great contrast to your present work sphere.

I suggest a meeting *in situ* with the possibility of a month's trial without obligation on either side.

While I realise you must honour your period of notice should you decide to join me, may I submit the urgency of my need. As, doubtless, Tom Lemon will have conveyed, this is a resident post and though I am myself sleeping on the premises at the moment family ties make it imperative that this should cease as soon as possible.

The practice is old established with a varied *clientele* and, though I do not speak without prejudice, the country hereabouts is kind. If you will be travelling by train I can meet you at Stroud or Kemble, if by road I will supply a sketch map.

Yours sincerely,
Kenneth Carr.

The address she already knew. It was simple: Butter Cross, Hopehampton, Gloucestershire.

There were unusual features. The word 'adverting'. The reference to the 'kind' country. The classical sentences. Obviously her prospective employer was a man who liked words and treated them well. Somehow you would not look for that in an overworked country vet. Middle-aged, of course. "Oh, you know, knocking on a bit, like me," Mr. Lemon had said vaguely.

She had expected Don to approve and he did. "You'll like it," he said confidently. "Very Charlotte country. And you'll have a flat, you say? Clever girl. We'll all be down for weekends."

At the supper table that night Ruth Lavender looked startled for a moment and then pealed with laughter. "What can I say, honey? I ran a whole lot farther after your dad."

It was natural that Mummy wouldn't have smelled the trouble because she never looked for such a thing and in her own experience had always ridden roughshod over it. But the remark was unfortunate. Yes, we're both runners, Charlie thought, but not in the same direction.

Her face put Ruth on enquiry. A mistake. She shouldn't have said that. "Poor baby," she thought compassionately. "That's my wonderful old mother-in-law with her Jane Austen mind. Why shouldn't a nice kid like Charlie show a nice guy like Don that she's committed? And why feel guilty telling me?" But Charlie *was* telling her. That was important. Even if she *was* trying to pretend that the main reason for the change was 'good experience'.

"At a lower salary, I guess?" Ruth moved her tinted specs and twirled them. Working as Charlie did in one of the largest and most modern city clinics she was earning the maximum salary a veterinary nurse could expect.

"I daresay," Charlie said coolly. "There's accommodation. That compensates."

"It's true." Ruth gave her daughter a long look. It could only be Don. A change of job must be on the map for him as well. She's my child after all, she thought warmly, she wants the things I wanted when I was her age.

"And haven't you forgotten something?" she prompted laughingly. "Where will Don be while you're swanning it in Gloucestershire?"

"Here, of course. Where should he be?" Charlie challenged composedly.

Ruth Lavender's blood ran a little chill. Good grief, had she backed the wrong horse? "Oh, my poor baby, she was mad about him," she thought pityingly. But her 'poor baby' had her at arm's length and she could sense was begging her to stay there.

Furthermore, Charlie was continuing that in view of Mr. Lemon's personal interest the hospital were releasing her at the end of the week.

"So soon?" Ruth looked vainly for a clue in her daughter's firm little face.

The letter from Mr. Carr was good-looking, nice writing, nice paper. To tell the truth, she hardly took it in. Have I done all I should have? she questioned. Don, for instance. Could I have helped her there? She's so much a Lavender, the old lady saw to that.

"What does Don say to that?" It was a cautious feeler.

"To expect him for a weekend." Not strictly true, but Charlie was letting herself down lightly. It would help to think that the door was not tight shut. A crutch, no doubt, but as yet she was not strong enough to walk quite alone.

But at that moment her mother laid down Mr. Carr's letter. "I'll miss you."

"*When?*" Charlie retorted.

It was meant as a compliment. The name of Ruth Lavender must have ranked amongst the most popular partygoers in the area.

Surprisingly the quip brought silence. Her mother's cheeks in the frame of long hair looked suddenly thin. One of her slender hands went to the side of Charlie's face. "I'm sorry, baby," she said contritely. "Honey baby, I'm sorry. Come for a weekend soon and I'll *be* here. All day.

That's a promise."

She said it again on Saturday morning at Paddington. "I won't even burn the toast, darling. I can't say fairer than that."

"Not just say. You couldn't not do it," Charlie returned unkindly.

The clock was at nine-fifteen and doors were slamming. It would not be the first time that Mummy seeing someone off had been literally carried away.

"Take care, honey," Ruth urged with a last hug. "Ring me soon."

"And you," Charlie cautioned, returning the hug. "Mind you don't go to sleep in the underground!"

That too had happened before. Sign of a relaxed mind, Mummy said airily. Be that as it may, her insistence on coming to Paddington this morning had necessitated getting up hours before her usual time on a Saturday. I know what she means when she says she'll miss me, Charlie decided fondly, watching a wilderness of steel snake past her window.

Mummy was a bit of a fusspot. "You have to change at Swindon. Don't forget," had been her final word. Sweet but bunkum. Charlie just didn't do that sort of thing. Her training had been too good.

Now she settled down to enjoy the two-hour train journey.

Almost immediately the other Charlotte took over. There had always been two Charlottes, the one who used her head and the one who listened to a very foolish heart. Years ago that one had looked at the stuffed fox and thought that it was asking to go home with her. Today, as the maze of tracks gave place to the suburban parks and gardens of Middlesex, it was just as dotty.

Don had not said good-bye. At the break-up of the farewell party last night he had taken her by the shoulders and looked into her face. "See you, Charlotte." He was the one person at the hospital who had never shortened her name. A friend had been driving her home. For a wild moment she had wondered what would have happened had she been walking to the underground. Most likely nothing, she had thought firmly, and had got into the car. They had passed Don on the road and he had waved at them and shouted : "Hi!"

The illogical Charlotte for whom Mary Lavender had trembled found it blissfully easy to believe that he had wanted to say more. Even the logical Charlotte—now that the moment was upon her—was having doubts.

Yesterday's farewell to four years of her life had been a greater ordeal than she had bargained for.

The animal hospital had been her first and only work sphere. She had come to it at seventeen with five 'O' levels and the words of her Careers mistress ringing in her ears. "Remember you must never get too fond of them. It's not a sentimental job."

Yesterday, however, all the old stagers had turned up for the afternoon surgery. Poodle 'Brandy' with his mistress who wore a black beret and kept the queue in line like a chucker-out. Labrador 'Hereward' back because his bandaged leg was swelling. Marmalade tom 'Little Chip' in his master's arms, his usual model of bored elegance, and nervy Mrs. Pohl who was Bavarian and charming but who never stopped looking at her watch and wondering if she could spare the time. "How I'll miss them," Charlotte thought as the train pulled into Swindon.

"Can you manage?" a young man asked across the carriage.

"Yes, thanks." Already she had womanhandled her case from the rack.

So far so good, and nice timing into the bargain. The message was already coming over the amplifier : "The train now arriving at platform three is the ten-thirty-six for Stroud, Gloucester Eastgate and Cheltenham Spa, calling at Kemble and Stonehouse." The platform was about fifty yards ahead and Charlie hurried towards it.

"Shall I carry that for you?" the young man offered again.

"Not worth it, thanks," Charlie laughed. "It's not heavy."

She gave the gallant a second glance, something most of her friends at the hospital would have done long ago. He merited it. He was dishy. Fair and very tall in yellow trousers. She noted a snuff-coloured jacket worn over a brown sweater, a yellow shirt and a gay cravat. He had a shapely face which for some absurd reason made her think of an ivory paper knife.

"It's a nice day," she added shyly.

"Very pleasant," he agreed. He had a beautifully pitched voice. "A good Cotswold day."

Ninety-nine girls out of one hundred would have jumped at the chance of further acquaintance. Charlie muffed it. When he stopped at the next carriage and said : "This all right?" she said confusedly : "Yes. Anywhere I'm not going far," and took the first available seat. The one beside it and the two opposite were already occupied. The implication struck her immediately, but it was too late. He had moved on. Oh dear, she thought remorsefully, he would think she had given him the brush-off.

Perhaps she should not be going to a one-man practice where obviously much would depend on personal relations. At the hospital numbers had pared this down. Just the same, yesterday had been full of surprises.

The news of her departure had leaked out and poodle 'Brandy' had said it with flowers, an African violet in a pot and a moist black nose on her hand. "Like I said, ducks, he'll miss you," Brandy's militant owner had declared. And like I said, *twit*, Charlie had told herself scathingly because of the sudden lump in her throat, you can be done without. She had not felt that way about all the patients, but there was the Skye terrier whom she had been hand feeding and who had had an operation that morning. She had slipped up to the in-patient kennels to see him before she left. He could not possibly have known her. He had "G.A." on his card and he was still comatose. He had looked—as he was —very ill.

She had turned away feeling not in the least like the celebration which had been arranged. There was a presentation in the shape of a new soft yellow suitcase and then three of the vets had taken a bunch of them across to the local for a drink. "And if he don't treat you right, honey chile, you let us know," one of the boys urged.

They were a great gang for nicknames. Charlie owed hers to the honey lights in her hair. She had always been a quiet one in a crowd; it was more than she deserved, she felt, that they should have liked her.

The train had run through a tunnel and into a station where it had stopped briefly. It was now on its way again.

The country was green and leafy. Horses and cattle grazed in the long fields. What else? Imagination sketched in the wildlife, squirrels, rabbits, foxes. All of them somewhere in the picture, they had to be. Picture or book? A book in green covers waiting to be opened.

"I like it," she thought happily. "It *is* Charlotte country."

It could not be far now to Stroud and Kemble where Mr. Carr was meeting her. She rummaged in her holdall for comb and compact and put on navy blue gloves and a navy blue high-crowned beret.

"We're just in," said a voice intuitively. The fair boy who had wanted to carry her case was on his feet moving down past her to the door. "Is this your station too?"

"Stroud?" As he nodded, she went on: "No. I go to Kemble. I don't think it's much farther?"

"Kemble?" His face changed. "You've passed it. It was the last stop."

"Passed it?" Charlie leaped to her feet. "It's *beyond* Stroud, surely?"

He shook his head. "I'm sorry. It was the last station. You didn't see the name?"

She hadn't looked. She had just taken it for granted. Kenneth Carr's letter had said 'Stroud or Kemble'. His confirming postcard had said merely: "I note you will come on the 9.15 from Paddington and will meet you at Kemble." Stroud—Kemble. It was too silly for words, but she'd just assumed it.

Anyone would have found it daunting. Charlie found it catastrophic. In her tidy well-mannered childhood mistakes were culpable. Her grandmother had taught her to memorise lessons and check change as though her life depended on it. And in the hospital a mistake could make all the difference to a patient's life. Today's episode was not a matter of life and death, but it was embarrassing and shaming. A busy man would have wasted time. "What will I say to him? What will he think of me? she thought despairingly.

"Cheer up. It's not as bad as all that," her companion

consoled. "The natives are friendly here. War drums in fact haven't been heard for years. It's quite safe to venture into the interior. You tell me where you want to go."

"Hopehampton," she said worriedly. "Is it far?"

"Nearer than Kemble, actually," he answered reassuringly. "So that's no problem. Anyway, I'm going there myself."

Charlie had had more than she deserved. She was aware of the fact but still depressed. Getting to Hopehampton was one thing, explaining her stupidity to Kenneth Carr quite another. She saw Stroud through a daze. It was a busy town with a traffic problem with which obviously her rescuer was well acquainted.

The car climbed out of it on to a road high above a valley. A harebell haze shrouded both dip and hill. She saw the soft outline of a town on the lower slopes. Nothing too sharp or abrupt. It was like a frieze full of blue enchantment with here and there a paintbrush blob of gold.

"Is that Hopehampton?" Charlie asked eagerly.

"No, that's Chalford," her driver replied. "Chalford and the Golden Valley. Hopehampton is much nearer. We're just coming on to the Common and then we're practically there. By the way, I should have introduced myself. Guy Wychwood. I'm the curate at Christ Church."

Charlie looked again at the belted yellow trousers and the peacock finery above them. And very nice too, she thought.

"I'm Charlotte Lavender," she said. "Once hoping to work here too, but now not so sure."

"Because of that muddle over Kemble?" Guy had an encouraging laugh. "I thought we'd settled that."

"Not to Mr. Carr's satisfaction, I fear." She stopped short. Undoubtedly the suede-clad shoulders beside her had twitched. "I suppose you might know him. Mr. Kenneth Carr. He's a vet."

"He has a higher honour than that," Guy confirmed modestly. "He's my brother-in-law. And I think we may say he leaves biting to his patients. May we also say that you're his new nurse?"

"How did you guess?"

"I'm gifted that way," he said modestly. "Especially

when I'm told in advance! I knew Ken was expecting you today." He waved a hand. "There you are—Hopehampton Common. We're nearly there."

Ahead a sea of green lapped at the road. It made another picture as the car bounced through. Brown and black cattle, horses and ponies with their foals, a terrier racing after a golf ball.

"Nice on a day like this," Guy agreed. "It gets foggy up here in winter. That's Tom Long's Post." He jerked his head to indicate. "It marks the place where they used to bury highwaymen." Houses and cottages were straggling into view. "We are now making our approach to the metropolis," Guy announced.

At that moment the sun came out.

Hopehampton had got into the Cotswolds by ten miles. It was just that distance to the western edge of the region. But it was very much in the club of honey stone and dormers. No stage lighting could have bettered the effect of sunshine on the pillared seventeenth-century Market House. The kerbs were high, the streets narrow, the windows small.

A book in green covers, Charlie had thought from the train. The book was now open. Fancifully, it seemed to be saying: 'Walk right in.'

"Oh, what a lovely place," she said, entranced.

"Do you know the Cotswolds at all?" Guy asked. "Hopehampton is a typical village. The stone, of course, is famous."

"It's like honey," Charlie opined.

She was forming a rough mind picture of streets diverging steeply from the market place when the car drew away from the road and mounted the cobbles in front of a bow-fronted inn. Again it was delightful, peaky-roofed and buff colour with its name on a signboard, the Chuckling Cheese. To the left of the entrance a pair of high wooden doors marked 'KEEP SHUT' effectually concealed what lay behind. Beside these a smaller door bore a bronze plate.

K. D. Carr M.R.C.V.S.
Veterinary Surgeon.

The Chuckling Cheese had been a coaching inn. Kenneth Carr had leased and converted the old stable yard. There were lofted buildings round two sides of the square. The nearest building had a glass door.

"This is the office. I'll go in with you if you like," Guy offered. He glanced at the empty cobbled yard "His car isn't here. He must have had calls to make on the way back."

Charlie had no doubt that this was a situation she should face alone. Guy had been cheery and restorative, but it was unfair to look for his protection. Besides, it was unbusinesslike.

"Thanks very much. I'll take this one on my own," she said firmly.

In the powder room of the Chuckling Cheese she checked her appearance. On the whole it was satisfactory. The French navy trouser suit with its buttoned pockets and flared turn-ups had a gamine air. The pale blue tie-neck blouse showed its long cuffs. She hitched her shoulder bag, re-settled her beret and took a firm grip on the new yellow suitcase.

The surgery hours displayed on the wall of the building included: Saturday 10–1, but when she tried the office door it did not yield.

Waiting at the best of times was a trying business. This was not the best of times. The clink of bottles and barrels from the precincts of the Chuckling Cheese played on her frayed nerves. When at last the timber door into the stable yard opened her heart gave an agonising leap.

It was not her would-be employer. It was a little company straight from a picture book.

A child in outgrown jeans and a Red Indian headdress, a slow old rough-haired terrier and a weatherbeaten elderly woman with a tweed cap worn peak aft. The woman had a fox round her neck. A live fox. Worn like a fur. Charlie stared. She could not believe it.

The child with the Indian headdress ran ahead. "This is it," she reported, and tried the door handle. When it failed to turn she rattled it with a vigour that made Charlie fear for its life.

The child was wispy with long brown hair that looked as

though it had not been brushed for a week.

Charlie was more interested in the fox. Remarkable as it seemed, it was the first time she had ever been close to one. The glossy brush was no surprise, but she had not realised the delicacy of the slim black-streaked forelegs or the tender white that outlined its mask. Nature was beautiful in its detail.

"May I stroke him?" she asked.

The woman did not reply. For all the notice she took she might not have heard. She had a face like cracked leather.

The child, however, was vocal. "Be careful!" she warned. "Don't hurt her. She's got a bad foot."

Charlie had not noticed the vixen's injury. Now she saw it. One of the hind feet had been torn and was suppurating.

"Martha is very clever," the child continued. "She cures lots of things, but we need penicillin here. Wouldn't you agree?" Not waiting for Charlie's somewhat dazed assent she instigated another assault on the door. Not surprisingly it did not budge. "I don't know what can be keeping him," she muttered crossly. "This is an emergency."

It became one at that moment. A lorry which had been standing outside the Chuckling Cheese started unloading, with deafening clangour, a consignment of metal kegs. The vixen, tame as she appeared, was not proof against it. She jerked, slithered to the ground and streaked across the cobbles. For the moment terror made her forget her wound. Swift as the wind, she went under the timber door.

The old woman watching her made a sound like an animal. If, as Charlie was beginning to suspect, she could not speak, the anguish in her eyes said all that was necessary.

It was a time for action. The dog and the little girl were already in pursuit.

"Don't worry. We'll get her," Charlie promised, and joined in the chase.

The Indian headdress was hovering uncertainly at the door of the inn.

"I can't see what way she went," its owner confided tearfully.

"You go up, I'll go down," Charlie panted.

The fox was running short and sooner or later it would have to stop and be cornered. She hoped that if the chance came her way she would have the courage to grab it.

Hopehampton was bigger than she had realised. Hilly streets went up and down from the Market House and there was a surprising amount of traffic. Charlie asked a man outside a greengrocer's if he had seen a fox. She did not wait for his reply, his gape of astonishment was enough. On the other side of the street two women came out of the hairdresser's and stood chatting. Suddenly one of them stiffened and turned her head. "That was a fox! Did you see it?" she was exclaiming as Charlie came racing up.

They pointed and in the distance, now limping badly, the vixen could be seen heading heaven alone knew where, but certainly away from the village centre. Charlie had run hard and was becoming short of wind, but hope put new heart into her. She had her quarry in view as she came out of the little shopping street and saw a gracefully towered church set in a green graveyard.

She could imagine how inviting that must look to the fugitive as she saw it rush across the road and disappear through the lych gate. For it too hope had taken over from pain and exhaustion. Here, she felt sure, it would go to ground.

With only one thought in her head Charlie dashed into the roadway. Next instant the screech of brakes pierced her eardrums. She pulled up, her heart thumping. She had neither seen—nor looked for—the car. It had obviously been travelling towards her from the left and now it was in the gutter, stationary, its offside tyres scraping the kerb.

"What the hell are you playing at?" shouted an angry voice.

It had every right to be angry. "I'm terribly sorry," Charlie said patiently. "I didn't see you."

"Try looking," the voice rasped. "And not so fast!" Her desperate movement towards the lych gate had not gone unobserved. "If my tyres are cut you're going to pay for them." A big dark-haired man was getting out of the car.

"Oh, I will. Naturally," Charlie gasped. "But first I must get the fox. It's in the churchyard."

"Not a bad place. The more dead foxes I hear of the better."

"I didn't say it was dead," Charlie flung back. "It's injured. They were taking it to the vet and it got away. I must find it." She thought his jaw dropped as she sped past him and through the gate.

Valuable time had been lost. The vixen was out of sight and had left no traces. Charlie searched anxiously, trying to keep calm. All hope lay in having her wits about her. The man had followed her and all of a sudden he waved. As she drew near, his arm described a circle. Not understanding in the least, she altered her approach. He was standing in a place where the grass was high and there was a tree. The vixen, patently exhausted, was lying behind it. The enemy had caught up with her; at that moment there was nothing she could do.

It did not quench instinct. As Charlie bent over her, her long jaws made an attempt to snap.

"Be careful," the man said irritably. "Well, there's your fox," he added. "Let's hope she stays there till I can put her down."

"No!" Charlie cut in, horrified. "I told you, she's going to the vet."

"Not if I know it." There was no bluster. He evidently thought that ended the matter. A farmer, she decided. Farmers detested foxes.

"You can't. It's not up to you," she pointed out. "If you'd only listen—this is a pet. It belongs to an old woman and a child and it got away from them in the vet's yard."

"Where *you* were?"

Of all the irrelevant questions! "Yes, where I was," she agreed tetchily. "Now will you let me take it?"

"I most certainly will not." A firm hand clamped on her arm. "Not even to feed your Orpheus complex."

"Let me go!" Charlie wriggled indignantly. "I don't know what you're talking about."

"You see," he said, pained. "First crazy, now uneducated. Orpheus was the mythical quasi-divine whose sweet music brought nature to his knee."

It really was insupportable. "Oh, shut up about Orpheus," Charlie flared. "The child could be under a car by now. I saw the state she was in and the way she was running."

Astonishingly it had an effect. The face changed. "Yes," its owner said thoughtfully, "there is that. Right, stay here till I get a sack. And don't touch."

What a man, Charlie thought, looking after the thickset frame as it strode away. In all her life she could never recall having been addressed in such an overbearing tone. It had not been necessary; she took such pains to be logical and controlled. Today, inside two hours of crossing into Gloucestershire, she had been caught up in an infection of carelessness. If you were superstitious, you could take it as a warning.

Who was this man, she wondered, did he live here, what fear was there of meeting him again? Plainly, he thought himself somebody and, truthfully, he looked it. About thirty. Short hair cut to show off a column-like neck. Clean-shaven face, defiantly classical. As were his clothes. The herringbone jacket was a made-to-measure job, the red tie brought up the black and white check shirt. He had immense shoulders. In a word he was 'Masculinity'.

"Born to boss," she thought grimly. "But not me, thank you very much!"

'Masculinity' had brought a sack which confirmed her impression that he was a farmer. He opened the mouth of it and put the vixen inside. She resisted, snarling, but he handled her well—Charlie had to give him that.

"Now then, let's be off," he observed, "before we're taken for grave robbers."

Unlikely, Charlie thought, with the fox's mask peeping out of the sack. She looked back fleetingly at the church which she assumed must be the one to which Guy Wychwood was attached. It was a decorative building with a clock in its tower. The tower was unusual, it tapered into a sort of stone mitre.

"Describe this child to me," her companion requested abruptly. "Did she belong to the woman?"

"I'm not sure." Charlie had been puzzled about the relationship. "She called her Martha, but she could have been her granddaughter. She wasn't unlike her, now I come to think of it, a real little ragamuffin, all her clothes were too small and she had a feather thing on her head like a Red Indian."

"And you think she's a vagrant?"

"Well, she spoke nicely, but I think she's living rough."

"I know her." It was unexpected. "I've seen her around," he explained in response to Charlie's glance. "I know the old woman too. She's harmless. She has a roost over near the Devil's Churchyard."

Charlie thought it a singularly apt address. In fact the association of ideas sent a shiver through her. By now they had reached the car which mercifully looked undamaged. Sack and casualty were placed carefully on a rug on the floor and she found herself hustled into the passenger seat.

"What is the Devil's Graveyard?" she asked.

"A place. Reputed to have been part of the 'old' religion in days gone by. Nowadays redundant. The devil has spread his wings. Were you at the vet's for treatment?"

"No, I ... it was a business matter," Charlie said hesitantly.

There was a pause. The car rounded the corner into a pale stone street. Looking sideways, she saw her companion smile as though he were licking his chops. His voice when it came was silky: *"Miss Lavender, I presume?"*

It was a moment she was to re-live over and over again. Shock and horror took her breath away. She stared.

"Kenneth Carr," he said briefly. "On my way back from Kemble. What happened?"

The carelessness had to be admitted. He listened, making a sound of surprise when she referred to his brother-in-law. "It's fortunate he was there. The buses aren't frequent." He ran the car on to the ramp by the Chuckling Cheese.

The double doors onto the yard remained closed, the small one was open. Through it old Martha could be seen sitting on the office doorstep. She looked like nothing so much as a pile of old clothes.

"You will treat the fox, won't you?" Charlie asked sharply. She could not bear to think of hopes being raised in vain. In fact she could hardly bear to look at the old woman. It was so pathetic and so tragic.

"I've told you no," Kenneth Carr stated uncompromisingly. "Hereabouts we don't treat foxes. One marauder less is a cause for gratitude. Not that in this case the beast won't be grateful too. It's suffering. It wants an end to its misery." He cast an eye round the yard. "I don't see the child. Where has she got to, I wonder? Let's hope you're not right about her running under a car." The anxiety in his face was undoubted—and warming.

The man after all was not devoid of feeling. More than that, he was worried.

"I'm sure she's all right," Charlie reassured him. "Children in her situation soon learn to look after themselves. They have to, poor little things. I'm sorry I alarmed you. Don't worry."

"Worry?" He was staring at her, the grim look back on his face. "Wrong again, Miss Lavender. I'm not worried, I'm itching to tan her backside."

"You couldn't. You have no right—" Charlie began positively.

"Four wrongs, I think," he pointed out. "Or have I lost count?"

She should have guessed his profession, Charlie admitted, as she watched him retrieve the sack from the floor of the car. It was evident that he had been trained to work with animals and logic made her admit that in the case of the vixen many people would support him. In the case of the child, no. The waif knew no better. As one of the 'have nots' of the world she had made a venture in faith. She had come trustingly to ask a favour. *Let this man lay a finger on her and so help me I'll* . . .

Ruth Lavender at home in Hounslow would not have known her daughter. Nor would the young vet at the hospital who had complained that she did not switch on. Charlie's cable system was near ignition point as they started across the cobbles. She had no heart to call to old Martha. Why pretend? This in effect was a funeral procession.

"I take it she can't speak," she whispered as they approached.

"Error number five," her companion returned. "She speaks when she wants to. Mostly it's done for her."

The words were barely uttered when a familiar small

figure darted into the yard. The child was still wearing her feathered headdress and the old dog ran beside her barking. She shouted a word which made Charlie blink.

"As I say, Sam the Mouth," Kenneth Carr remarked. He stopped as the small figure hurled herself at his waist.

"Where was she, Daddy? Where did you find her? She got out under the door. Did that person tell you? She was helping me look. Oh, gosh!" she fanned herself. "I'm not able to speak. Have you seen her pad, Daddy? She needs penicillin. Martha couldn't lock her up and the cut opened. I said you'd want to keep her and Martha doesn't mind. So is that all right? You can take it out of my money."

"Samantha," Kenneth Carr did not raise his voice, "go and sit in the car."

The child had an insignificant face. It was pale and it peeped through the maze of hair. Charlie forgave herself for this final gaffe. No one would ever have taken her for 'Masculinity's' daughter.

"Do as I say, Sam," he was now repeating.

She looked distressed. "I want to watch. I want to help with her. She knows me."

"You will be helping." Charlie was surprised by the moderate tone. For a man in a dilemma no trace of it was showing. He now turned directly to the apparent bundle of rags on his doorstep. "Go home, Martha. The fox won't suffer, but she must stay here. If she doesn't she'll die. Even if she does she may die anyway. But without pain, that I promise."

"Daddy!" Samantha Carr was not after all as insignificant as she had seemed. Her eyes, more green than blue, were quite beautiful. Charlie, who had never had much success with children, found her evocative. She was about seven, all arms and legs and hair, and something terrible was happening to her. She was no longer sure that everything was going to be all right. Charlie's heart ached for her as the question wobbled out: "*You are going to give her the penicillin?*"

Kenneth Carr's eyes were a solid blue like lapis lazuli. They did not flinch.

"Yes, Sam, I'm going to give her the penicillin," he said evenly. "Come, Miss Lavender, please. Enough time has

25

been wasted as it is."

Charlie, following him through the waiting-room to a small well-lit surgery, tried to depress the soaring of her spirits. It was unlikely that the vixen had been reprieved. She knew an iron will when she met one.

"What did you mean?" she risked diffidently as Kenneth Carr laid the sack carefully on the floor.

"What I said," he answered curtly. "Work it out."

The casualty, weak from her struggles, was now much quieter and the musky fox smell not nearly so strong. She was caged and injected without trouble.

By now Charlie had decided where all this was leading. "I should have thought it cruel to prolong life when there's no hope," she submitted.

"Don't sound so melodramatic," the vet said briskly. "I know what I'm doing. At least the beast will be fed and rested and soon out of pain. The penicillin will see to that. There's nothing for you to do at the moment. I merely brought you in to explain. Sam is a problem which my circumstances don't help."

"Your circumstances?" Unethical perhaps, but the words slipped out.

"I was about to say. My wife died when my son was born. That will soon be two years ago." It was a tone carefully purged of emotion. "A rarity, thank God, but sometimes even today the thing one never dreams of happens. Well—that's by the way, except that it forms the nucleus of my arrangement with you. As you can imagine, it has been difficult to be two parents. I had hoped that with someone here on whom I could rely I'd have more time to devote to my home." The pause spoke volumes.

"Of course. I understand." Charlie's bright colour had deepened. "If you could direct me to the station I won't take up any more of your time."

"Not so fast." The large face looked amused. "I'm trying to convey my difficulties, not asking you to add to them. I know you're bad on trains and foxes, if you're good on cats and dogs you could still be useful." He glanced at his watch. "Come and see your quarters. While you're settling in I'll run Sam home and then we'll continue the discussion over lunch."

"It's kind of you," Charlie began awkwardly. "But really I don't think I'd suit."

His eyes flicked over her hot cheeks. "Possibly not, but then you're not coming as a suitor, so we needn't cross that bridge. Try to be more adult, Miss Lavender. It's not compulsory for you to shine to me. In fact I'm not in the market."

At the least it was unexpected, at the most it was detestable. It took total self-control not to hit back literally at the poised lip and the smile.

"That was uncalled for, Mr. Carr. You knew what I meant."

A change swept over his face. "Yes. I apologise. However, let's not be irresponsible. Both of us have made an effort to get thus far. Surface dislike shouldn't prevent the month's trial we agreed on."

It made sense, and there was Mr. Lemon. Charlie doused her anger. Did she really want Mr. Lemon to think she had lost all sense of proportion? Besides, truth struck hard. It was her carelessness that had caused the first confrontation. In justice to Kenneth Carr, he had set out in the character of his courteous letter to meet her and buy her lunch.

"Oh, Gran!" she muttered. She often thought of her grandmother and used her name like a talisman.

Unhappily the wretched man was staring at her. "What?" he asked politely.

She was quite sure he had heard. Too silly. Only a child made up exclamations. It made her blush. "Very well," she said firmly, "I'll stay. On the understanding I'm not committed."

For a second he seemed to be hiding a smile. Then his eyes went grave.

"Of course," he returned emphatically. "That has never been in dispute."

CHAPTER TWO

SIXTEEN years ago a fox had earned Charlie a telling off, now another one had repeated the process. Happily it seemed that her new employer was not going to remember it for as long as her grandmother had done. As he took her case and ushered her into the yard the atmosphere was considerably more relaxed.

Charlie was receptive to places. With this one she could not better her first thought, a page from a picture book.

Practical as the conversion had been—and no one could fault Kenneth Carr's architect on the layout of surgery, operating theatre, X-ray unit and kennels—the restored eighteenth-century façade was sheer delight. The new stone was creamy against the warm honey of the Chuckling Cheese. Archways from the courtyard gave access to the various units. Dark blue balconies projected from what had been the loft doors.

They passed under one of the archways and came to a narrow dark blue door. This was opened and a staircase was revealed. "Up you go," she was bidden.

The flat was newly decorated and charming use had been made of plain and contrast walls. The sitting-room, mostly green, went from sprigs of harebells to narrow stripes; the bedroom from a clovery shade to a wall of pink cornflowers.

The furniture was not new, but like the exterior had been lovingly restored. A blue glass lamp with a tall chimney sparkled on a golden pine chest of drawers. In the sitting-room a sturdy Victorian chair had been refurbished in sheeny dark green; there was a white cased wall clock and a couple of interesting old tiles hung on wire plateholders.

" 'Junk' buys most of them," Kenneth Carr said carelessly. "Now and then you're lucky." He looked round. "I hope you'll be comfortable. You must tell us if there's anything you lack. And by the way there *is* plenty of soap and water!

"If you like that kind of thing," he added at the door.

It had not closed before Charlie was in the bathroom gazing in horror at her reflection—cap slipping off the back of her head, dust on her trouser legs, a long smear on one cheek. Drat the fox and drat the man! It was the second time he had laughed at her.

She had to be content with what was at the top of the case, a short tartan pinafore in navy blue, pink and gold, a navy shirt with a touch of swagger to it and navy tights.

"I don't want to come all the way up again," her host had said gallantly. "Meet me in the Cheese."

"Are you sure you're not busy?" she had countered diffidently. "I can easily get something for myself."

"Not at all," he had assured her. "I'm relishing it."

It made more impression than if he had said 'I'm looking forward to it'. But right from his first letter she had judged him to be a man who loved words. Conversation with him could be refreshing. Some of her own richest hours had been spent with books. They were not the riches Don had brought, but they had been utterly free from pain.

As she stepped out into the shadow-patterned courtyard and closed the door behind her everything seemed welcoming. Here in this picturesque backwater she would enjoy watching the rest of the world go by.

In sunshine the Chuckling Cheese made a mellow pile, first the older and simpler public bar, honey-gold with age, and next the hotel with its Gothic window moulding. The inn sign, a round smiling-faced cheese, hung over the old inn, an antique coke brazier stood at the entrance to the hotel.

She was the first to arrive and after she had waited in the foyer for about twenty minutes her happy mood subsided. Unfair to blame him, she knew, there could have been an emergency. "I'm sure I'm being a nuisance," she thought. "I should have said no. Why didn't I?"

The swing doors parted and for the nth time she looked up. Disappointingly the entrant was a girl. One, however, at whom you would look twice. Dark hair with brown lights in it tossed as she walked. Accented eyes, very dark, peered from a canvas hat. Her colour scheme, mostly yellow and shocking pink, had been put together admirably in trousers, shirt, cardigan and a rope of beads.

Charlie had got as far as thinking 'Italian tourist' when the newcomer spoke. "Good afternoon, Peters." She had caught the eye of the hall porter. "Is there someone here waiting for Mr. Carr?"

Charlie, rising hesitantly to her feet, was met by an amused stare.

"*You?* That's a laugh!"

It took the wind completely out of her sails. Suddenly she knew how wrong she looked—short dress, long legs, little rosy. In fact, fresh out of kindergarten. "I—er–" she began, and was immediately talked down.

"I'm Jasmine Buck. Mr. Carr told me you'd be waiting. He has a mountain of things to do today, so I said I'd take one at least off his hands."

It was shock, disappointment and horror, mostly horror.

"It's very kind of you," Charlie owned quickly, "but it's not necessary. Please. I can look after myself."

"No. No. No, I insist." The dark head shook impatiently. "Car's at the door."

It was indeed. It was bright orange with a flashy boot.

"Here we are," its owner said briskly. "In you get. If you don't mind I'll just feed you and run you back."

"Miss Buck, please." Charlie stood irresolute with her hand on the door. "I do wish you'd count me out. Really I do."

"Oh, get in. Don't keep me waiting," the other retorted quickly. "I'm on the yellow lines."

It could have been put more gently. Charlie flushed. It did not go unnoticed.

"Now don't tell me you're offended," her driver said lightly as she edged into the stream of traffic. "In Woodsgift we call a spade a spade. You'll have to get used to that."

Perhaps there was truth in it. Perhaps she had been over-sensitive. Worse still, had she displayed her resentment over the lunch date? An innate something warned Charlie that she was being assessed—probably the way with all small communities when a stranger came amongst them. Certainly the moment for her to keep her cool.

"Woodsgift?" she echoed as the car plunged steeply downhill. "Is that a village?"

"No, it's where we all live. My father and I have the big house, we bought it from Mrs. Wychwood, but there are three other houses as well. She and her son have one, Mr. Carr has another. Handy, that, since he usually gets me to entertain for him—as today. He sent you his excuses, by the way. I know it's disappointing, but he's a very busy man."

Not too busy to talk about it, Charlie thought, not too busy to moan and have her taken off his hands. Oh, really! It was a ridiculous situation. She would have infinitely preferred to be on her own.

Resentment choked her appreciation of the drive. She was conscious that the road dipped and climbed, leaving the cottage gardens on the outskirts of Hopehampton for fields and greenwoods and a National Trust sign. At the end of a long hill the car swung sharply right over a cattle grid beside a white wicket. She had not expected anything so private and it was so full of interest that she felt like begging her driver to slow down.

The upswept drive overlooked on the right by the woods had on its first bend a white Georgian house. Thereafter, it snaked to the left and the full charm of Woodsgift came into view. To the left was a hollow and the sound of water.

"Mrs. Wychwood's territory," Jasmine Buck said briefly. "I warn you she doesn't like trespassers."

Charlie, craning to see down from the car, had to be content with the top of a dovecote.

But already her eyes were looking ahead delightedly to two honey stone houses each on a fork of the snake's tongue. Each had the Cotswold character she was beginning to recognise—buff roof tiles, pointed gabling, oak doors. One had a terrace over a car port, the second was more of a family house. A German Shepherd snoozed by the hall door and the big beds in front were bordered with Cotswold stones and soft with roses.

The car swung away from the houses, first right, then left, and stopped. This time there was no question where they were. 'My father and I have the big house,' Jasmine

Buck had said.

It was a big house indeed and a striking one. It had been colour-treated in a strong shade of olive, window frames and down pipes were dazzling white, door and shutters a vivid daffodil yellow. Charlie had no doubt it was smart, but she could not help thinking it would look better in a town. The other houses blended so kindly with the beech woods and the undulating fields.

"Oh, can't you open it?" Jasmine Buck enquired. "The door. It lifts up. And I see the milkman has been. Take the bottles, will you. Careful," she added warningly. "That's my lot till Monday."

The warning was timely. Out of nowhere, or so it seemed, a dog had come dashing. Charlie, startled by the onrush, just managed to save the bottles.

"Oh, Nicky, you are a *menace*!" Jasmine expostulated, slamming the car door.

The dog barked about them for a few minutes, his slightly domed occiput and soulful eyes contrasting with his tail which was going like a rudder. He was a beagle.

"Yours?" Charlie questioned.

"Not on your life!" Jasmine retorted. "He belongs to the domestic."

Curiously enough the dog's owner did not seem to be in evidence. The kitchen into which Charlie had followed somewhat diffidently held no other occupant. "Does she live in?" she asked.

"Lord, no," Jasmine was putting the milk into the fridge. "She's just a char. Pretty hopeless, but all I could get. She's gone to the doctor, actually, and the sooner she gets back and removes that pest the better!"

It sounded ungracious, but was probably meant to be a joke.

"Anything I can do?" Charlie offered.

Jasmine had thrown off her long belted cardigan and her hips had an animal grace. She wore her dark hair soft, brushed back and swinging like a bell. It was thick and glossy, almost Spanish-looking. Her silk shirt rustled and was precision-tailored. You wouldn't have bought it under twenty pounds. Charlie tried not to be envious of the shirt. She had a weakness for nice separates.

32

Nicky had padded off upstairs after putting his paws on the drainer and snatching a piece of chicken, for which he got his nose slapped.

"Oh, *blast*!" Jasmine exploded. "Yes, take the cucumber. My hands are full."

It was not the easiest of meals, though the food was excellent and set out modishly on a circular plate glass table. However, as the courses proceeded, the atmosphere became more relaxed.

"Oh, call me Jasmine," Charlie was commanded. "Surnames are a bore. What does one say to you?"

Charlie, who had been thinking that it seemed like vandalism to put a spoon into the blackcurrant water ice with its garnish of whipped cream and strawberries, came down to earth. "Most people say Charlie." Don who always said 'Charlotte' was a long way away from this room but somehow not so far from Jasmine. A crazy thought, perhaps, when they had never met, but there were people whom instinctively one's mind put together.

And the memory of Don still hurt.

She felt it was typical of her hostess that although she probably found this piece of entertaining a nuisance everything continued to be done well. For coffee they moved from the dining end of the large open plan room.

"Do you think you'll stand living in the country?" Jasmine asked. "Hopehampton can seem like the grave after London. I speak from experience. Of course you won't have my disadvantages. You're not living in Jean Wychwood's old house. It took a long time for her to swallow our buying it, she hasn't digested it yet. You see, we don't belong to the peerage. That's all the old witch thinks about these days—my name for her. Rather apt, don't you think?"

It was embarrassing. Charlie smiled uncertainly.

"She's away at the moment," Jasmine continued. "Holidaying with one of her aristocratic friends. In fact she troubles Woodsgift very little, I'm thankful to say. Ken is at least spared her interfering with the children. Now that Marjorie is dead they might as well not exist. Marjorie was different, a bore but harmless. Oh, of course, you don't know who I mean. Marjorie Carr, Jean's

33

daughter and Ken's wife. It was through Ken we bought this place. He told me it was on the market. Candidly I don't think his mother-in-law will ever forgive him, but candidly I think he has always found her *hysterical*. He likes us being here, of course, he'd like to think I've put my roots down permanently, but it's difficult." she shrugged. "These damn woods give me the creeps at night."

Charlie was starting to get the picture. Jean Wychwood, the widowed ex-owner of the manor, now living at its gates presumably with Guy. In one of the other houses, Kenneth Carr, her son-in-law.

"And the fourth house?" she asked diffidently.

"The old man's sister has it. He made it over for her retirement. She's a teacher, I mean used to be. You'll probably like Steph. Not my sort either, I'm afraid." She waited a second. "Will you stay?"

Three words. They echoed as Charlie blinked. "I suppose so. If I'm kept!"

"Ah! You mightn't be. Ken was furious, you know." The lips folded so that a dimple showed. "You're much too young. He wanted 'a settled person'!"

It was like Kenneth Carr to be arrogant. And it was infuriating.

"What does my age matter?" Charlie demanded. "I'm a Registered Animal Nursing Auxiliary and I have my certificate to prove it."

"Worn next the skin, I trust? Or in the teapot with the wedding lines?" Jasmine asked teasingly. "Oh dear," her dark eyes widened, "I've done it again. You're offended. I must warn Ken you can't take a joke."

Charlie knew it was silly to feel hurt, but repartee was a game at which she had never been good. Her cheeks flamed.

All in all the visit had been something of a trial. It was a relief when Jasmine announced without preamble: "Well, that's it. I've got work to do now so I'll take you home."

Nicky's bark sounded as they went into the hall. For want of a better word it was 'round'. Mellow. It really sounded exactly like: Wow wow.

"Where *is* he?" Jasmine questioned irritably.

He was on the landing looking down on them from above. He was beautiful, hazel eyes, big nostrils, close hard coat, round feet. When he saw Jasmine he ran downstairs, his tail going side to side.

"Oh, shut up! No!" she snapped. "You can't come. Go for a walk."

Charlie was sorry for the dog and a shade apprehensive. "You haven't got some safe place to leave him?"

"Safe place?" Jasmine looked amused. "You're a bit mixed up, my child. I'm not responsible for him."

Charlie sensed that she had offended. "Please don't take this amiss, but from where I work you see the other side. And sometimes it breaks your heart." She was thinking of the open exit from the drive to the road.

"Tut-tut," Jasmine mocked. "You don't know your lines —or your future boss. Non-involvement, mouse, that's the success story." The dark eyes so skilfully outlined and shadowed looked sideways for a second.

Charlie supposed it was the thick walls of the house that made the hall suddenly seem so chill.

A glance round as they went out to the car re-impressed the manor's idyllic setting. Nothing could have been more peaceful than the wide lawn that washed away from the front door. To the left the view was open and pastoral with a few Friesian cattle on the hill. To the right the woods were so densely green that it was like looking in under water.

"I suppose you're smelling the garlic. Ghastly, isn't it?" Jasmine asked as she switched on the engine.

"As a matter of fact I was being covetous," Charlie said honestly.

"I do believe that's a sin," her companion observed. "And it's a funny thing about me—what I have I hold."

Really Jasmine was awkward company. Everything she said was jokey but peculiar. You'd be better keeping your mouth shut, Charlie told herself, and at that moment opened it again in a cry of pleasure.

When the car had been climbing up from the entrance she had not been able to see into Mrs. Wychwood's hollow. Now facing down from the plateau, it was exposed. The white dovecote stood by a lake. A lake at the bottom of a green hollow. As the car flashed past she saw a seat and a little statue and three white doves swooping brilliantly across the summer sky.

Next moment to her astonishment the car's speed slackened.

"Now what?" Jasmine questioned.

The tall fair-haired figure striding towards them waved a hand. It was Guy Wychwood. "Hello there!" He turned to Charlie. "Nice to see you again. Everything work out all right?"

Charlie said: "Fine," and received a disarming response.

"Good. Can I invite you to tea tomorrow at my aunt's house?"

"Oh, don't mind me," Jasmine murmured. "My favourite role. Juliet's nurse."

"And *don't* mind her," Guy ordered Charlie. "Will you come? I know Stephanie—my aunt—will be delighted."

It was a temptation, but one should learn by experience. She had been palmed off once already and most uncomfortable it had been. Tomorrow's proposed incursion, this time into the Wychwoods themselves, could be even worse.

"No, thanks. If you'll excuse me," she said gently. "I need some time to myself to get my bearings."

"Tactics, mouse. You're improving," Jasmine remarked as they drove on. "You handled that very well."

Used as she was becoming to enigmatic comments, Charlie started. She had been thinking of Guy's disappointed expression and hating herself.

"I wasn't handling anything. I don't know what you mean."

"Oh, come on! You were playing hard to get. And no bad thing," Jasmine opined thoughtfully. "If you play your cards right Jean might let you have Guy, she says she's looking for a wife for him." She grinned at her passenger's gasp of anger and bounced the car over the cattle grid.

The shops in Hopehampton were still open and as soon as Jasmine had driven off Charlie headed for them. The thought of her little flat was welcoming and a spur. She hurried home with her purchases and unpacked both them and her suitcase. Then she went downstairs to see the caged fox. It was still asleep, curled up like a cat with its brush wrapped over its muzzle. There were no other in-patients.

It was so still. Not a car, not a motorbike, not a human voice. She heard the tick of the wall clock all over the flat and once or twice the cooing of pigeons on the roof of the hotel.

She walked round her domain for what must have been the tenth time and studied the tiles on the sitting-room wall. The most interesting one showed a strange animal with a red, black and white horn standing on what looked like a chalice. It had puzzled her the first time she had looked at it and it continued to do so. Gran would have known, she thought. To a little girl growing up there had seemed to be nothing that could best Mary Lavender. Her tall spare figure with the carefully husbanded smile had been not unlike a pillar.

Yet Gran, who had been a widow living alone, must often have been lonely and felt much less than the tower of strength they had thought her. Tonight she seemed near because tonight the one thing Charlie had never allowed for had happened. She was lonely. Gran would have had the answer to that one. 'Find something to do.' Gran, of course, would also have thought that coming to Hope-hampton had been running away.

"And truthfully, Gran, from where I'm sitting," Charlie thought, "I've run from the frying pan into the fire." In point of fact she was sitting on the stairs. It was one child-hood habit Mary Lavender had never succeeded in eradi-cating. "You'd wash your hands of me," Charlie added, resting her cheek against her knee so that a piece of hair flopped forward and tickled her nose. "Oh, Gran, I shouldn't have come."

The thud hardly penetrated because by this time trade was perking up in the Chuckling Cheese and outside it car doors were opening and shutting. She didn't even bother to look up until she heard:

"Miss Lavender, have you—Great Scot, is something

wrong?"

Her head jerked like a nervous filly. The hallway below her was narrow and it seemed to be completely filled by the man who was staring concernedly up the stairs.

"No, Mr. Carr." She scrambled to her feet.

"Are you alone?" He looked past her to the landing.

"Of course."

"But you were talking to someone."

"No." She shook her head.

"I heard you." He stood by the newel post as though he was the counsel for the prosecution.

The most appalling suspicion flashed through Charlie's mind. She damped it down. "Did you want me?"

The decoy was ignored. "Then you must have been talking to yourself." His blue eyes were deepest under wing-shaped brows. They pinned her.

Charlie repeated her question: "Did you want me, Mr. Carr?"

The test of any face is how it looks unsmiling. This one had style. The lightly tanned features might have been set in bronze. He would look well on a plinth, stern, clean-cut and unfriendly.

His voice was matter-of-fact. "Yes. I've got a cat here. Can you give me a hand?"

The cat, a long-haired marmalade, did not look ill. Its light green eyes were round and clear. It had been missing since the previous evening and had dragged itself home an hour ago apparently on its forepaws. When Kenneth Carr lifted it out of the basket, it tried to run, and the sight was heartrending. The hind legs wobbled and crumpled to the floor. Terrified, it scrabbled a few paces and fell over again. This time it lay there, thrashing its tail and panting.

"Did you say it got home *like that*?" Charlie was picturing the nightmare journey.

"Must have done. What's more, the garden has a wall round it." The cat's owner had not seen it negotiate the wall. She had discovered it exhausted on the path. She was middle-aged, single and living alone.

"The cat must . . ." Charlie saw where she was heading and broke off. No point in inviting trouble.

."Yes?" Kenneth Carr enquired.

"I was going to say 'must love her'."

"And you don't think I'd agree?"

"I.think you'd—find it—absurd."

There was a pause. "Then I suggest you work on it," he advised.

The man was impossible. "I'm sorry. Work on what?"

"Your understanding of me. It seems to have got off to a remarkably bad start."

Charlie had to clamp down on the temptation to retaliate in kind. The eyes seemed to be enjoying her struggles.

"Mine of you is more precise," their owner added. "Shall we for instance stop pretending that there's any comparison between predatory vermin and a fine cat which I have every hope will mend."

It was safer to think only of the cat and how deeply she shared that hope. A first examination revealed that it had all its reflexes. Charlie's mind went to a pelvic fracture. Kenneth Carr nodded.

"Or it could just be disc trouble. I don't think he's been knocked by a car. There are no cuts and his coat is clean. Well, no use conjecturing. Let's find out."

In every working relationship there has to be a first time. Charlie was to look back on this first assignment with satisfaction. Kenneth Carr, whatever his defects as a person, was a good vet. His hands were skilled and gentle, his manner kind. He went to great lengths before he was satisfied with her positioning under the X-ray machine.

"So far so good," he reported after reading the plate. No bones were broken but there was a spinal haemorrhage, possibly a burst blood vessel which had clotted and was causing pressure on a nerve. The treatment was rest and cortisone injections. After a day or two they would know more.

"He's a climber, this cat," the vet remarked, filling a syringe. "Goes up trees. My guess is he fell out of one."

"I've seen birds turn on a cat," Charlie submitted.

"So have I." He daubed expertly and the needle plunged.

One thing after another had exhausted the patient. It

39

stiffened for a second against Charlie's bare arms making the rough harsh purr which she had learned over the years could be a sound of pain. She gentled it, trying to find a spot which would give pleasure. "You're beautiful," she thought. "Get better, lovely cat, get better and *walk* home."

Her employer glanced at her as he pulled down his sleeves. "Thanks. Keep an eye on him, won't you? I'll be in tomorrow to give him another shot. He can have food if he'll take it. Most likely he won't. Anyway, you're not a greenhorn, you'll know what to do."

She nodded. No one in their senses could call the remark a compliment, but, strangely, it did make the world seem a friendlier place. Or at least it made Charlotte Lavender feel more like her usual competent self.

She knew that she had now neither need nor desire to return to her perch on the stairs.

Kenneth Carr had left a parcel on the table. When she drew his attention to it he gave her a studied look. "Rabbit —for the fox. And for Pete's sake be careful. Drop it through the top of the cage."

Tim (Kenneth Carr had confided that this was the cat's name) was soon sleeping off the effects of the injection, having drawn himself as far into his basket as he could. It was his own basket from home and Charlie imagined he found it a comfort. The person she would have liked to comfort now was Tim's mistress who had not heard the more hopeful prognosis. Her name was Roberts and she lived in Lime Tree Cottage. "Just at the top of Well Hill," Kenneth Carr had said curiously. "You pass it going to Woodsgift."

Charlie could not rid her mind of Miss Roberts. Her employer with his policy of non-involvement might not be too pleased, but a few more blots on her copybook at this stage would be unlikely to matter.

Lime Tree Cottage was easy to find. It stood just below the crest of the hill and its garden ran up from it like a streamer. The elderly lady working there could only be Miss Roberts.

Not surprisingly, she responded warmly to the call. In minutes Charlie found herself occupying a chair and being plied with lemonade. When under pressure she agreed to a refill of her tumbler there was a slight hiatus.

"Which was your glass, dear?" her hostess asked doubtfully. "I've got in a muddle. Mr. Carr had one too, you see."

"Mr. Carr . . ." Charlie was astonished. "You mean . . ."

"Your Mr. Carr. He's just gone. Oh, never mind," Tim's owner was rambling on. "I'll get you a clean one. Wouldn't that be best?"

"I hadn't realised Mr. Carr would call," Charlie began awkwardly.

"Yes. Wasn't it kind of him?" Miss Roberts beamed. "Just like you, dear, and just like his grandfather. Old Mr. Carr was a wonderful man. He had the practice for fifty years and nothing was too much trouble. Miss Stanley helped him and she was exactly the same. But I didn't expect young Mr. Carr . . . well, I mean, these days you have to carry everything, don't you? They ask you to. But I don't have a car, I don't even have a proper basket and of course it was long after hours. But the moment Mr. Carr heard about it he was round. I'm sure it didn't take him more than five minutes. And then he even came back to tell me it mightn't be as bad as it looked."

All in all Charlie felt decidedly foolish and all of a sudden very tired. It was only ten o'clock, but the day's adventures had taken their toll.

She looked in once more on the animals, checked that she had not left any doors open and went to bed. She must have dropped off immediately and awakened almost as soon—ten minutes, to be exact. She checked her watch under the bed light. Somehow she was uneasy. Something had roused her. What?

She sat up, listening. Yes, there was a sound. A small sound as though something was scraping on glass. A heavy sleeper would not have heard it, but Charlie had always slept lightly.

"What do I do now?" she thought, and answered herself. "You dial 999, chum. Someone is trying to get in."

There was no need to panic because the intruder, whoever he was, would fail. She had herself deadlocked the doors leading to the surgery and the flat and she knew from the demonstration Kenneth Carr had given that it would

41

be impossible to push back the nose of the bolts. The windows too had special screw fasteners and they were in place.

At the same time, it didn't help to remember that Jasmine had said about getting the creeps at night.

"Don't be daft," Charlie told herself again. "There are no woods around here." But there *was* a pub. Someone must have got smashed.

At this point the situation changed. First the door bell went and then the knocker. It had an effect on Charlie— mad fury. She pulled back the bolt on the french window, ran out on to the balcony and looked over. "All right!" she shouted. "I'm not deaf. What do you want?"

It was not yet dark, but dusk had fallen and dusk is a spooky time. Spookiest of all was the figure lurking in the shadows. It had jumped when Charlie called out and now it took a shambling run across the courtyard. Truth to tell, it looked more like a bear than a person.

Well, of course, it wasn't a bear. Charlie took hold of herself as the figure halted and came back. The face shone up at her, a blob in the twilight. The gappy mouth, however, stayed dumb.

"Martha!" Charlie expostulated. "What are you up to?"

She had to answer her own question. Martha was silent. She looked witless, but Charlie had no difficulty in understanding what was in her mind.

"Yes, she's still here," she said firmly. "Mr. Carr looked at her foot and gave her an injection. That's all he was able to do today. Martha, I promise you, she's quite safe. Go home." It should have ended there, but there was something about her battered old face that, as before, went to her heart. "You want to see her, don't you?" she echoed compassionately. "That's why you've come?"

For at least a moment of complete silence their eyes held each other, Charlie's sapphire blue ones young but very direct under their smudgy brows, the old vagrant's well washed with rain and grief.

"He said she was harmless," Charlie thought worriedly. "So—will I? What harm could it do?"

What she would really have liked to do would be to give her something to eat.

"Martha, she has to stay here, you know that," she repeated. "Her foot must be cleaned out, properly. It's been closing and opening again for weeks, hasn't it? But so long as you understand and go away quietly I'll let you in, just for a minute. I've decided."

Undoubtedly the old woman heard, but not a muscle moved on her cracked face. Charlie flung on her dressing gown, thrust her feet into slippers and went downstairs. The light snapped on in the passage and immediately Martha's dark shape moved down to the surgery entrance. Charlie opened the door.

Her first thought was how much worse the old creature looked with the light on her, her second a very chilling one. Martha had come from the Chuckling Cheese, and not without sampling their products. She was also considerably bigger than Charlie had realised.

There was nothing for it but to draw back.

"Why don't you go home now? Come back tomorrow and we'll know more."

For answer a large rough fist went to the jamb of the door.

"No, Martha," Charlie said firmly. "I'm sorry. I didn't realise. It's too late."

Fool that she'd been! The fist just shoved that much harder and the door moved. Charlie, tall but narrow, hadn't a hope.

"No, Martha, no!" she gasped. Brute force took on a totally horrible clarity. If Martha got inside she could cause damage.

It happened quickly. One minute she was engaging all her strength, the next it was over. There were footsteps, a shout, and stronger hands grabbed the assailant from behind. Male hands and sinewy male wrists held Martha at arm's length. Kenneth Carr's blue-stone eyes went grimly to Charlie's face.

"Who opened this door?"

"There's only one person who could have," Charlie said tartly. "I'm not afraid to say so. It was me."

"I," he corrected.

She bit her lip in vexation. Of all the pedants! She would treat that one as it deserved.

"She was making a nuisance of herself?" he darted.

"She wanted to see the fox."

Kenneth Carr's face froze. "She can do more than see it, she can remove it. And she's lucky if I don't prefer charges." He shook the tattered sleeve he was holding. "Now listen to me, Martha. You're not such a fool as you look. You've tried to cure the beast and you've failed. You know what will happen if you take it away, don't you? It will die. The poison will spread and it will die, in great pain. Now you go away and think about it. Come back when you're sober. And if ever I catch you trying that on again . . ." There was no need to finish. Martha was already shuffling across the yard.

Charlie waiting could hear her own heartbeat. More disturbingly, she could see the curve of Kenneth Carr's jaw.

"Did you say something, Miss Lavender?" he asked abruptly, and added : "Curious," as Charlie's head shook. "I should have thought you would have had some explaining to do."

She could expect no less, but the panic she had felt over Martha was nothing compared to that which possessed her now. And suddenly, despite the high frilled collar on her dressing gown, she was deathly cold.

"I'm sorry. I under-estimated her," she said miserably.

"As apparently I over-estimated you," her employer retorted. For a second his face changed. "Are you all right?"

She had hoped her shivers would pass unnoticed. It was a shock reaction. Idiotic, and the last straw. She tried to nestle into the sprigged cotton of her dressing gown; unfortunately it was a garment for modesty rather than warmth and her flushed cheeks must match its pinky orange flowers.

"Perfectly," she stuttered.

"I can see that," he returned. "Now don't faint on me. After the day I've had I couldn't stand it. There's no brandy, but I'll make tea—and don't think you're going to wriggle out of the row, because you're not."

"I've no intention of wriggling out of anything, and I don't want tea," Charlie said angrily.

"Sorry about that. You're going to have to drink it.

44

And to listen to me."

It would have been satisfying to refuse the tea, but the purposeful way in which it was put before her seemed to brook no argument. Besides, it was very hot and the cup warmed her hands.

Kenneth Carr lifted a chair across and straddled it.

"Jasmine tells me you like to be called Charlie. I've no objection. I'll use anything that will make an impression. You're not what I hoped for or what Tom Lemon led me to expect, but you do represent a challenge. Yes, what is it?"

Charlie had let her cup into the saucer with a rattle.

"I haven't finished. What is it?" he repeated.

"Nothing," she said dazedly.

"You succeed a very wonderful person." His voice had softened. "Nora Stanley. For forty years she all but ran this practice. At the moment I find myself very much like the woman who prayed to be cured of bad temper and was sent a bad cook." He hesitated. "If you see what I mean?"

"Oh yes," Charlie said earnestly. "I'm glad you prayed about it." It was cheeky, but at least the flames would be bright as she went down. "Will you take my notice now?" she asked quickly.

"Will I *what*? Have you heard one word I've been saying?" He looked toilworn, there was a spot of disinfectant on his collar and his hair was awry. "No one is taking notice or giving it," he went on roundly. "I can see you'll be a liability to start with, but I'll turn you into an asset if it kills me. It may kill *you* first, of course, but we must risk that."

Charlie's mouth opened indignantly and closed again incredulously as he continued : "One thing we won't have time for is ceremony. The name's Kenneth—Ken if you prefer it. You may ask as many questions as you like, but you may *not* argue. It was one rule I always followed with your predecessor."

"And I suppose she never ever broke it?" Charlie smiled wanly. Just her luck to have to follow a paragon !

The face confronting her creased as though in pain. "The next time you're talking to your grandmother *in the dark on the stairs* ask her what she thinks of that revolting

45

double adverb. It offends me continually."

The words pinged into the silence. They shattered her.

"I don't talk to my ..." she broke off guiltily. "Well ... only ..."

"Now and then. When the going's hard. I know." It was an extraordinary gentle tone. Next instant his voice sharpened, pulling him back, she felt, from the past. "Now you go to bed. Fresh start in the morning. I'll check that old vagabond isn't still hanging about." At the door he looked back with a grin. "In case you're interested, your predecessor was not under duress. The rule was for *my* protection. Cheerio."

CHAPTER THREE

THE morning was bright. A chaffinch perched on the balcony rail as Charlie made her breakfast. It was a friendly gesture which Tim, alas, would not emulate. He still drew fastidiously into the recess of his basket and made it plain that he endured her hand only because he could not run away.

The vixen was awake and watching her.

"You got me into trouble last night," Charlie said reproachfully.

Kenneth Carr had not given a time for his call on Tim and she decided to go to church. Inside, as well as out, the building had grace. She liked the painted bosses on the ceiling. A boy server in a red cassock put a taper to the candles on the altar.

The service was orderly. The choir processed in surplices and blue cassocks, the servers followed them. Guy bringing up the rear looked too tall for his short surplice and his longish, slightly curly hair was a medieval touch.

The choir came in both sexes and practically all sizes. A rosy-cheeked little girl sang with abandon, opening her mouth like a fledgling in a nest.

> We worship you, we give you thanks,
> We praise you for your glory.

The surprise came when the collectors clattered into the aisle, because they were all children. And one of them was familiar—that is, when you looked the second time. Yesterday a ragamuffin, today—bless my soul, what a dog's dinner !

Samantha Carr had just about everything bar the kitchen sink. Her hair was caught at each side with two enormous red bows. She had a brightly patterned dress and a poncho that was all colours of the rainbow. She also had lacy white socks and a pair of new brown sandals and she was walking on her toes.

Who bought her clothes? Charlie wondered. They all looked new and they were not without a nod to fashion, but they were wrong for their wearer and that made it pathetic. She was staggered at the gush of pity that swept her, especially as no one could have looked more pleased with life than Samantha herself. The smile never left her face even when some coins slipped off her plate. Down she squatted, looking a bit like a tent, and the child behind her in the procession all but fell over her.

Charlie wondered if she had come to church unaccompanied, but towards the end of the Communion she spotted the two red bows again. They were going up the aisle and behind them Kenneth Carr was driving a blond toddler by its upheld arms. The toddler was small. Its white socks reached to its chubby knees and it was inclined to strain forward so that the pale blue coat went up and the pale blue pants came down.

Kenneth Carr prodded it on like a donkey and together with the gorgeous Samantha they came to the altar rails.

Charlie could not understand what came over her, but somehow she wanted to cry. The tiny boy did not kneel, he stood quite quietly between his father and sister, resting his pale blue sleeves on the rail. Guy's hand stayed lightly on both small heads, the round primrose one and the beribboned brown. She fancied his look was sympathetic.

Samantha's for her little brother was certainly so. When the little family rose to its feet she took one of his hands protectively into hers. Father and daughter passed Charlie's pew with the youngest member toddling between them. Unexpectedly father smiled.

"I don't know why I never thought of them as being happy," Charlie thought stupidly.

When, subsequently, she made her way out again into the sunny churchyard the trio still holding hands were talking to a lady near the door. Charlie trying to be unobtrusive, felt a touch on her arm.

"Just a minute," her employer commanded. "You haven't met my son. My daughter you already know," he added as Charlie bent delightedly to the children.

"This is Jason." Samantha was still beaming. "But we usually call him Jay. Did you see him in church? He was

48

very good."

The man of the moment was enchanting. He had long dark fringes to his blue eyes and the same winging brows as his father. He started to smile and incredibly that too was Kenneth's, small and roguish. But shortlived. He jerked his head away, laying it against his father.

"I'm afraid he's at the shy stage," the lady remarked. She was middle-aged, wore glasses and country clothes and had a pleasant smile. She included Charlie in it.

"You haven't met either. I'm sorry," Kenneth apologised. "Stephanie, may I present Charlie Lavender. You knew she was coming. Charlie, my good friend, Stephanie Wychwood."

"Oh yes," Charlie acknowledged, shaking hands. "Guy mentioned you yesterday and so did Miss Buck. You have a Norfolk terrier."

"Yes. I had hoped you'd come and meet him this afternoon," Stephanie Wychwood submitted.

"Stephanie," Samantha put in earnestly before Charlie could answer. "Would you like us to come instead?"

"Now you see why we call her Sam the Mouth," Kenneth Carr observed. "Duty calls," he added. "Steph, you'll excuse us, I'm sure. Menagerie, forward march!" He swung Jason into his arms, poked Samantha in the small of her back and motioned Charlie to follow.

She did so feeling dazed.

"Where are we going?" she asked as the car door opened before her.

Answer was prompt. "A woman's work is never done. No more is a vet's. I want to look at this cat."

The children were not allowed into the surgery. Tim, lifted out on the floor, appeared to Charlie to be no better. He made yesterday's scrabbling rush and subsided. Kenneth Carr said: "Hm," and put him gently back into the basket. "I'll give him a shot. He won't try to walk much while he's in pain."

It was a dexterous operation. The Sunday look of brushed hair, lightweight suit and blue and white pin-check cuffs remained unruffled.

"Is he eating anything?" The cat's plastic feeding dish came under scrutiny.

Charlie's head shook miserably. She was disappointed. She had made up the meal with great care.

"Not to worry. Perhaps it's not his advertised brand."

"It is." Charlie had taken care of that. "It's some Miss Roberts gave me. I thought it might tempt him."

"Miss Roberts?" he stared. "When did you see Miss Roberts?"

"I went round—I'm sorry. I was afraid you mightn't approve."

"Mightn't approve?" The eyes had picked up the colour of the air-force blue suiting. They were puzzled. "I see. My flinty heart again." There was a momentary twinkle. "Well, don't jump to conclusions."

So far so good, but Charlie's hopeful glance towards the other cage was not successful. "I was wondering ..." she began. Last night's portion of rabbit had been small and had been eagerly if warily devoured. She had no more to offer.

'You never give up, do you?" Kenneth Carr commented. "But you know the score."

He opened the car door and Samantha shepherded Jason into the back and got in beside him, arranging her poncho so that she did not sit on it. Charlie, turning away amusedly, caught her employer's eye. For a second his brows went up. Then he said briskly: "Well, I've a dinner to cook. Thanks for your help," and slid into his seat.

Samantha waved as the car drew away and touchingly Jason copied her. The last Charlie saw was the top of his primrose head bobbing about in the window.

Kenneth Carr drove a dual-purpose estate car, teal blue and very long. That afternoon just as she was setting out for a walk she was astonished to see it glide to a stop beside the inn. When she retraced her steps Kenneth was unlocking the double doors to the yard. Her mind flashed at once to an emergency.

It was not that. Since the vixen's paw would be a long job he had decided to tackle it while he had time.

"That means ..." Charlie broke off. As always, his face was unreadable. "Let me put it this way," he corrected himself smoothly. "If you're available it will be a valuable research exercise for you.

"Have you ever thought about taking up research?" he enquired affably as they passed under the archway. "It's a responsible and rewarding field."

Charlie answered honestly. She had the greatest respect for the research department in the hospital in London, but knowing that animals had to be put down after operations had proved too much for her sensibilities. She accepted the humanity of the rule, but could not live with it, day in day out. Her own greatest joy was the reunion between patient and owner.

"Not only do you never give up, but you say the wrong things. Continually," her employer remarked.

The operation proceeded. The vixen was given an injection and then carried into the small theatre for a general anaesthetic.

"If you've ever been to the hospital at Regent's Park," Kenneth Carr observed, "they'll have shown you their anaesthetic boxes. That's what we need now. A wild animal can't stand up to shock like a domestic one. This one has had two injections. It could die. You must be prepared."

Charlie could have retorted that a fox which lay round its owner's neck could hardly be classified as a wild animal, but she thought better of it.

Even if his motive was to educate rather than to heal he was so skilful that soon his hands became the whole scene. Charlie passed swabs and scissors, and kept forceps and sutures ready. She realised now why the vixen had been denied food that day.

The paw had been opened and cleaned and now the cavity had to be obliterated by suturing. At last it was all finished and the patient bedded down on fresh straw.

"Now I'll ask you another question." Kenneth Carr was pulling off his gown. "Did you ever feel like being a vet?"

If the query had come from the motionless patient Charlie could not have been more surprised. "Feel like—yes. But I know my limitations."

"Funny." It was a dry tone. "I'd have said your wishes were quite unlimited."

Charlie was tidying up, dropping soiled dressings into the sanibin, collecting the instruments for sterilising. She looked up to find his eyes on her face.

"I was just thinking that since I've destroyed your afternoon you may as well have tea with us. Sam will appreciate another woman to talk to."

Two things happened. Charlie's heart leaped for joy; she would love to see the children again. Then it subsided. It was essential not to be a responsibility.

"It's very kind of you. May I thank you and say no?"

"Taking you by the buttonholes, as they say, because you have something better to do?" He was disconcertingly direct.

"Not precisely, but I'm sure you have," she said firmly. "I can look after myself."

"Yes," he pulled a smile, "I've had some examples of that. Come on, Charles, take it between the eyes. You can, I'll guarantee it."

"Take what?" She was bewildered. Could he by any chance have heard about Don?

Kenneth Carr's face was wooden. "My cooking. What else?" he retorted.

Charlie had been wearing jeans. She had put them on for the solitary ramble she had planned. They did not seem right for Sunday tea with the boss. "*What?*" she thought fussily, searching through a collection of blue and cream separates that were blessedly interchangeable.

In the end she plumped for a blue pleated skirt, a blue shirt with a white spot and a cream tank top. She used a pale raspberry lip colour and a warm blue eye pencil. Her hair, silky but thick, flopped boyishly across her brow.

Kenneth Carr had put the instruments into the steriliser. He had also locked up. "In case I seem overbearing," he remarked, "rest assured I won't commandeer you every Sunday. But if my wife were alive she would certainly not allow you to spend your first one in solitary."

It was a little dashing, but the reference to his circumstances she could not let pass. "It must be very difficult for you," she said sincerely.

"What must?" he asked curtly from the other side of car.

Charlie could not but feel that she had trodden on dangerous ground.

"Doing without her," she said lamely. "Especially when the children are so small."

"Now that, if I may say," the key turned and the engine started to purr, "is a typically female remark. I do hope, Charles, you are not a typical female."

To her mortification Charlie felt herself blush. The antipathy which had been stifled during his brilliant work on the fox began to rise again.

"I console myself in the thought that typical or untypical you dislike me," Kenneth Carr went on, oblivious of the pause. "This dear old town is full of those who want to marry me off for the sake of my children. However, it's an unethical conversation. Let us truncate it."

"Mr. Carr," Charlie inserted coldly, "you have nothing to fear from me."

"Thank you, Charles. You have a penchant for stating the obvious," he returned lightly. "Oh, there are problems, of course, I don't deny it. But thanks to my friends and relations I manage very well. I have an excellent home help Monday to Friday; weekends I stagger myself. The main thing is the children are at home and I'm bringing them up. Of course the hospital is a different matter. You are essential there, or someone like you. I can't leave kennel patients unattended at night."

Did he know what he had just implied? After all that had happened was he *really* expressing confidence in her? A slip of the tongue, she decided, with sad honesty.

"Which leaves me one last point," he employer went on as the car breasted Well Hill and passed Miss Roberts's cottage. "Your reason for coming and your feelings about the job. Think carefully now, it's important."

"My lettter explained," Charlie said flatly. "I wanted to work in the country."

"And that's all?"

Well, she was certainly not going to tell him about Don. In any case it made no difference. "Absolutely," she said firmly.

Though it was only the second time she had been there, the white wicket at the bottom of the hill already seemed welcoming and as the car bumped over the cattle grid the low-set lop-eared form of Nicky the beagle came bounding to meet it. Kenneth Carr palmed the horn and shouted: "Scat!" through the window. Nicky put his head on one side and looked reproachful.

"Confound it, he's still watching for Mrs. Green." Charlie hardly recognised the soft concerned tone.

"Who's that?" she enquired.

"The heroine of yesterday's debacle. Why look so surprised? You knew I took her to hospital."

Charlie was thinking quickly. Nicky belonged to Jasmine's 'domestic'.

"I knew she went to the doctor."

"Understatement," he commented wryly. "She had a heart attack. Just here, as a matter of fact, on her way down from the Manor. I came on her as I was setting out. An unfortunate set of circumstances all round. I phoned for the ambulance and, would you believe, it had just had a crash itself, so rather than wait for the replacement vehicle I took her in myself. It was one risk against another, of course, but all was well. Stephanie came with us."

Not Jasmine, Charlie noted. She would have expected Mrs. Green to have felt more at home with her employer. But perhaps not.

"I had no idea," she submitted.

"No?" He dismissed this easily. "I expect you got the wrong end of the stick."

It was insult to injury. She had *not* 'got the wrong end of the stick'. Jasmine had said nothing about an emergency. She ... all at once Charlie got the message. Such a crazy message that it was all she could do not to laugh.

Jasmine had implied that Kenneth Carr had asked her to help him out with the lunch date for no particular reason. What had been her motive? The conclusion could only be described as comical. Charlie's lips twitched.

"May one share the joke?" a voice asked beside her.

Horrors! No! "There isn't one," she said quickly. "I was smiling at Nicky. Will his mistress be all right?"

"I hope so, yes. Better if she could stop worrying about *him*," Kenneth Carr replied.

Charlie had had a preference for the family type house that stood broadside on to the drive and she was pleased to find that this was the Carr homestead. The wealth of pink and yellow roses she had already noticed, today's closer look showed what looked like an old arch in the stone above the door. As the long car swung round and into the garage the black and tan German Shepherd which she had also noticed yesterday stretched himself and came down the steps from the hall door.

In contrast to Nicky, the *enfant terrible*, this dog had made no attempt to run at the car and now it walked with the fluidity that characterised its noble breed.

Charlie knew that a German Shepherd does not fawn. Added to that, in this case, was obviously excellent training.

Kenneth Carr gave his dog a look of pride. "Paw, Max," he commanded. It was immediately proffered and taken by a delighted Charlie.

It struck her that the dog matched his master. "Messrs. Masculinity", she thought flippantly. Undoubtedly, the gold brown eyes were summing her up just as the blue ones had done yesterday. She trembled a little at the result. "I've seldom seen such a beautiful dog. He makes me feel inferior."

"Then you must stop feeling that," Kenneth Carr retorted. "It's at the bottom of all your muddled thinking. However, you've heard one sermon already and I don't want to spoil the day."

It was unexpected. Charlie looking up found that the blue eyes could smile. "It's a long time since we entertained anyone so pretty," their owner said gallantly.

Valiant efforts, he assured her, had been made in her honour. "Samantha, as you'll see, has made the old home a bower of flowers."

It was only too true. Every wide windowsill held a crammed vase. Some of the roses were beautiful, some from the yellow climber had been snatched off with tiny stems. Top marks for pathos went to the harebells, the herb robert and the already wilting poppies which had plainly been gathered far afield and carried home in a hot little hand.

She thought: "Supposing I hadn't come?" She said: "What a lovely welcome! She couldn't have done anything I liked more."

The silence was unexpected. After it came Kenneth's apologetic voice:

"I couldn't throw them out."

"Oh no!" She was horrified. "They *are* beautiful. The thought makes them so—I mean it."

Perhaps it was the sunwarmed room that made her cheeks burn and perhaps the colour in his was similarly a reflection of the sun.

"I'll tell her what you said. It will please her," he said quietly.

The children were over with Stephanie in the house on the common loop of drive. Bobby, the little brown Norfolk, sat on its terrace behind a wire gate.

"Sixty seconds to blast off," Kenneth remarked. "I asked Steph to hang on to them as long as she could, but Sam will be beside herself once she's seen the car."

It seemed odd that he should have wanted to delay the children's arrival. Charlie could only think apprehensively that another lecture was in store. It did not, however, materialise.

"He meant that about not spoiling the day, he really is treating me like a guest," she thought somewhat dazedly as she was offered a drink. "And he's so different," she thought five minutes later.

Kenneth Carr was explaining about Woodsgift. His late father-in-law had been an architect and when he bought the manor house had set about converting and improving the other buildings on the estate. Stephanie Wychwood's house had been the gardener's cottage. "And this one," Kenneth said smilingly, "was made out of the stable block. You probably saw where the top of the old door used to be and we have a mounting block. Unfortunately the best *we* can do for it is a clothes horse, but Guy has the genuine article. He keeps it by kind permission on Jasmine's land. My father-in-law," he added, "gave Marjorie and me this house as a wedding present."

It was providential, he continued, that Stephanie had moved into her house just when he needed her. She had a lifelong experience of children and Sam and Jason loved her. The bird table outside the kitchen window had been her idea and had provided hours of entertainment.

"Miss Wychwood is really their great-aunt, isn't she?" Charlie asked.

"Oh yes, but she doesn't look like it," her host said boyishly. "And they always call her Stephanie. I've been wondering if I should do something about that, but she insists she enjoys it. Sam calls everyone by their Christian names, I'm afraid. Do you mind?"

"Oh, Mr. Carr, of course not! I hate being called Miss Lavender," Charlie said warmly.

"Then take your own medicine. What did I tell you last night?" he challenged with a twinkle.

The remark coincided with the sound of voices across the drive. Kenneth grinned ruefully and pointed. As surmised, Stephanie was seeing the children off; a joke seemed to be in progress between her and Jason; Samantha, strangely, was showing no signs of humour.

Charlie had no idea what was afoot, but she felt concerned. Samantha's cheeks were as red as those unsuitable bows on her hair. Stephanie should see that and stop laughing.

The moment did not last. Nothing could come between Samantha and her duties for long. Jason was toddling off and she retrieved him with a practised hand: "Were you running away without saying thank you?"

The scene was typical of both children. Jason, short on speech, was strong on charm. He put up his face to Stephanie like a rosebud. Samantha watched approvingly and Max, recognising the signs, loped forward to bring them home.

It was a magic afternoon. Jason bounced on his father's knee to the tune of *The Galloping Major*. He walked up and down the garden between Charlie and Samantha singing *The Grand Old Duke of York*. Samantha sang atrociously; she was plainly tone deaf. Jason was spot on, his tiny treble was as sweet as a lark.

When Kenneth joined them and began marching too, picking up his feet and swinging his arms, it became hilarious. "I don't believe it," Charlie thought again. Kenneth had a fine voice, it was a joy to hear Jason's mingling with it.

The garden of the Carr house was screened from the

drive and ran back to the woods. It was a private garden with a hedge between it and Jean Wychwood's house, but it was in the flight path. The eight Wychwood doves made ceremonial swoops on the chimney stack and cooed in the summer air. A blue-winged jay screeched out of the woods. A missel thrush stopped off to eat a worm.

"And we have dozens of grey squirrels. They come for their breakfast, don't they, son?" Kenneth appealed to Jason.

"Sometimes they sit on our bird table," Samantha put in.

Something about Samantha still caused Charlie concern. Jason was a natural star. His hair grew in a round cap, his knees were sand gold. But oh dear, Samantha was not the type for that fussy dress with its red and gold flowers, its long cream sleeves, its lace centre panel and all the gewgaws of gilt buttons and scarlet ribbon. "I'm sure she chose it herself, and it *crushes* her," Charlie thought. Dress apart, the child's beautiful green eyes were lost in the straggly hair.

"Who wants tea in the dining-room?" Kenneth asked his offspring.

"*We* don't," they returned stoutly.

"Who wants tea in the sitting-room?"

"*We* don't!" The chorus was louder this time and obviously a family game.

He looked mischievously at the guest. "Who wants tea in the kitchen? *All together now!*"

Charlie accepted the invitation. "*We do!*" she yelled with the children.

The kitchen was square and large and pale green. There was a round white table and chairs. A robin sat on the bird table outside the window. Samantha pulled down the blind to display the green birds that patterned it. Then she bustled Jason away to the bathroom.

"Well, Charles, you've just passed your A-Levels. Tea in the kitchen," Kenneth announced, filling the kettle.

Charlie's eyes had been following Samantha propelling Jason gently upstairs. "She's a real little mother, isn't she?"

"Yes. It's meat and drink to her," he agreed, laughing. "That's my trouble. When it gets out of bounds there's no

58

knowing what it will bring in. I'm lucky if it's only a fox. But I confidently expect the day will dawn when the surgery door will open and Sam will walk in with an elephant!"

No one could have looked happier than Samantha at tea. She buttoned Jason's bib and steadied his mug of milk. When he looked like giving up she coaxed the last piece into his mouth. After the meal they all went into the woods to show Charlie where an old fox had made a lair for himself last winter.

"How soon will you come again?" Samantha begged.

"Well, I . . ." Charlie hesitated.

"Don't make yourself a nuisance, Sam," Kenneth interposed swiftly. "I've told you that before."

A reproof for Samantha or a hint not to take advantage of the child's invitation? Charlie was wretchedly uncertain. In the same moment Max's ears pricked, a twig cracked and Nicky broke cover. Behind him sauntered Jasmine.

"Well, look who's here!" she said lightly. "Hello, Ken." A graceful gesture swept aside her dark bell of hair. She put up her mouth and kissed him.

He showed not the least surprise.

"I want to talk to you," he said easily, and shifted Jason who was riding piggyback. "Can we do something about this dog getting on to the drive? He seems bent on killing himself."

Jasmine's eyes widened. "If he does, darling, that's perfectly all right by me." She linked his arm affectionately.

"I know it's an imposition," he conceded. "But do your best for me, just till I can make some arrangement. He means a lot to her, you know."

"Not as much as you must mean to me!" Jasmine sighed. She looked at Charlie, who had dropped behind with Samantha. "What about you, mouse? You must feel the fatal attraction too. I mean, you told Guy you wanted to be alone today. Or have I got it wrong?"

"Predictably," Kenneth said cryptically before Charlie could reply, "I don't know about Guy . . ."

"Oh, but I do," Jasmine cut in. "Poor Guy, he was so disappointed. However, is it in order to say the best man won?"

"Neither in order nor truthful, but don't let that stop you," Kenneth commented without annoyance. They were coming to the edge of the woods and the going was less rough. He set Jason down and encouraged him to walk.

Jasmine immediately took the little boy's hand. "Hello, greatest, you come with me."

Jason evidently liked her, for he trotted off at once, peeping back triumphantly at the rest of the company. When they reached the Manor garden he toddled over to a flowerbed, pulled the head off a marigold and presented it to her.

"Jason!" Kenneth admonished sternly. "You are not to do that."

"Spoilsport!" Jasmine reproached, poking the dimple in Jason's chubby cheek. "Thank you, gorgeous. You'll be twice the man your father is.'

Even at two-minus praise is sweet and discernible. Jason plodded over, grabbed another marigold and presented it, this time with a kiss.

"You see!" Jasmine said proudly.

Samantha too had her share of attention. "And how is the eldest? My favourite little nurse. Are they treating you right?"

Samantha had been on tiptoe, awaiting the chance to speak. It was evident that when it came to favourites she returned the compliment. Now she burst out indignantly: "Stephanie isn't. She made fun of me when I sang. I don't mind, of course, I just think it's terribly rude."

"Oh dear," Charlie thought. She had not been wrong. This was the reaction she had suspected when she had watched from the window.

"Steph used to teach music," Kenneth said to her quietly. "It's all right, Sam," he added. "It's not important."

"But I *can* sing. Listen," his small daughter urged, and forthwith opened her mouth.

The sound was horrible—and pathetic. Jasmine, however, did not bat an eyelid. "Indeed you can," she said with vehemence. "You sing beautifully."

Charlie could not have said that. She could not even be sure whether it was wise or not. But certainly it had its effect. Samantha's beam threatened to split her face.

Charlie found it a most poignant moment. There was no doubt that she herself had been completely eclipsed. Jasmine now had both children swinging out of her hands.

"She must be the number one favourite," she remarked to Kenneth, taking pains not to sound envious.

"She has a way with her," he replied lightly.

Another popular person was Guy, whose arrival at that moment was greeted by Jason with a bumbling rush. Guy caught his nephew goodhumouredly, smacked him and then glanced at the company. His jaw dropped when he picked out Charlie. "I thought you didn't want to come out today."

"I didn't . . ." she began in an undertone. "At least, I . . . Oh, it was too bad! Kenneth was staring at her in a way that could only mean he had overheard.

"The lady means she must do what the boss tells her," Jasmine took over deftly. "So why not kiss and make up, Guy, and then you can drive her home. All right, Ken? You won't object?"

"In heaven's name, why should I object?" Kenneth returned. He turned to Charlie irritably. "Go with Guy by all means, if that's what you'd prefer."

Guy was in jeans and a striped shirt. "With you in five minutes," he promised Charlie. "I have to change."

In very little longer he was back, dressed in clerical garb and with a damped-down look to his hair. Evensong would be starting in twenty minutes.

"Sorry for the rush," he apologised as they drove. "I was with Hannibal and forgot the time." He went on to say that the horse was now fifteen years old, his wind was gone and he was no longer fit for hunting. Jasmine had allowed him to stay on in his old pasturage. Apparently, though the Manor was owned by Jasmine's father, Mr. Buck was very seldom there and left all such matters to his daughter.

"It's not everyone would have been so accommodating. I wish . . ." Guy began ingenuously, and bit his lip.

"Yes?" Charlie prompted.

"I was going to say I wish Mother wasn't so down on them," he admitted naïvely. "I know she misses the old life and the big house, but I sometimes think she forgets the price she got for it. However, that's not your worry."

"I think my boss is worried about Nicky," Charlie submitted. "It would be dreadful if anything happened to him."

"Agreed. But Ken expects too much of Jasmine. She's a city bird. It's no use his thinking she'll stay here long-term, because she won't."

"Isn't it convenient that you were appointed to this parish?" Charlie asked, changing the subject.

"Very, but let's not make any bones about it. Mother knows people and strings were pulled." He had almost embarrassing honesty. "It's not right, of course, and I shan't stay too long. I just want to see her a bit more settled before I take off."

Charlie toyed with the notion of going to Evensong and put it aside on the strength of the kennel patients. She felt dispirited as she let herself into the surgery. In all conscience it was absurd, for she had had a full and for the most part an enchanting day. Jasmine alone had grated.

Am I just being bitchy? Charlie asked herself. It was a common failing with people who were not exactly candles to moths. Jasmine was a candle, a lithe, sinuous candle with a look of wide-eyed innocence.

Spurious, thought Charlie.

But she had to admit it was a ploy that worked. Guy thought Jasmine accommodating and Kenneth seemingly was hoping to persuade her to stay permanently in Woodsgift. It did not need much intelligence to answer that particular 'why'.

Meantime, she had more important things to do than brood over those that did not concern her. The vixen was starting to come round, twitching in the way that animals do when coming out of general anaesthetic, and Tim was beginning to look positively bright-eyed and bristly.

"Notice I didn't say 'bushy-tailed', you're that already," she told him. "Now come on, gorgeous, give me that breakthrough. Eat!"

Still no use. She patted the totally unresponsive cat, left it fresh milk and went.

CHAPTER FOUR

NEXT day work began in earnest. It was only three days since Charlie had last worn her uniform dress, a purple and white striped cotton, but it seemed like weeks. She clasped the black buckram belt round her slender waist, put on clean cuffs and apron and gave a final brush to her hair.

She was already in the surgery when Kenneth arrived. He stopped short in the doorway biting his lip. Charlie swept him a dark blue glance and went on sorting index cards. "Good morning, Mr. Carr."

"Good morning, Charles," he answered, laying down his case. "Do my eyes deceive me or has the tone of the place gone up an octave or two this morning?"

Past admonitions made it an opportunity not to be missed. "If you're talking about tone, ears would be more correct."

"Touché!" he conceded. "And felicitations. Keep trying and some day you may speak the English language."

Charlie thanked goodness for the interchange. It had wiped out yesterday's uncomfortable leavetaking. "I'm afraid these cards are in a shocking state," she said with a return to business. "They look as if Jason had been having a go at them."

"His father did," her employer admitted cheerfully. "The man is quite impossible. Haven't you always known it?"

It was a busy day, but there were no emergencies and much of the treatment was preventative, puppies for inoculations against distemper and hardpad and kittens for F.E. vaccination. There was a tabby cat with 'flu and another with mouth ulcers who commanded all Charlie's holding skill while its teeth were being scraped. In the lunch break Kenneth made two calls on farms in the vicinity.

Before the afternoon surgery began he made a further examination of Tim, who had raised Charlie's hopes by lapping milk but was still adamant about solids. The haemorrhage in the spinal cavities had ceased, but his walking powers remained at nil.

"I think I might send him home," Kenneth observed. "He won't do here. He's fretting.

"You don't think there's permanent damage?" Charlie felt the dreaded possibility could no longer be swept aside.

"I think we have a very sore cat and not enough patience. Even if we also have our cuffs on and starched at that!"

Next morning she heard the car arrive while she was at breakfast. It sent her downstairs at the double. Perhaps there was an emergency which would require her presence. Kenneth, however, had not entered the building but was rummaging in one of the outside stores. He came out in triumph with an empty tea chest and greeted her typically: "Good morning, Charles. Caught with your cuffs off, I see!"

The tea chest was for Tim, who was to go home that morning. Kenneth had explained to Miss Roberts last night that he would have to be kept quiet and had suggested some mode of confinement. She had nothing suitable, so he had promised to search round his own premises.

"So far so good," he remarked, tipping the dust out on the cobbled yard. "And nothing for you to do at this stage. Go back and finish your breakfast."

"Would you like a cup of tea?" Charlie gave the invitation on impulse.

It was accepted promptly. "That's an idea. I would."

She tested the teapot and found it good and hot under its knitted cosy. Kenneth sat down and she fetched another cup and pushed over the toast rack.

"What did you do with yourself last night?" he asked unexpectedly, and listened sphinxlike to the news that she had hired a television set and had seen it installed. "That doesn't sound very exciting. Does Guy know?" At Charlie's start of surprise he amplified the question. "I only mean, he's in touch with all the organisations at the church. You should join some of them."

Charlie was taken aback. "I'm not sure I want to at this stage. I'm not a lonely person and I'm looking forward to settling in."

"I appreciate that." His look was kind. "But at the risk of being told off may I say that's not such a good idea. I don't want to think of you sitting here night after night with the TV."

"Yon don't have to think of me at all," she submitted mischievously. "And this *is* my life."

"A very much younger life than I anticipated," he countered. "And I may as well not beat about the bush. It's giving me second thoughts. I don't think it's good for someone your age to be alone, and at the moment as you know I haven't the facilities to do much about it."

It had been a beautiful morning. The sun had wakened her and the window space had framed honey-coloured chimney stacks and a limpid blue sky. Now it was ruined. He was as good as telling her not to depend on visits to Woodsgift. As if she would! It hurt very much.

"I can only repeat—please don't worry about me. It's not necessary. I like my own company."

"Oh well," he shrugged, "I suppose that's plain enough. At all events we can't talk now."

Charlie was astonished and pleased to be given the job of taking Tim home. It was a trifle nerve-racking since he had found his voice and he yelled raucously all the way. There was certainly nothing amiss with his lungs nor, in one sense, with his backbone, for the moment his basket was lowered on to home ground he made his first voluntary attempt to leave it—a gallant if ungainly one. Out he flopped, scrabbled across the floor and hauled himself by the forepaws on to a chair by the window.

It was embarrassing to see how draggled and unkempt he looked; staring-eyed and matted, with sawdust in his coat, but to groom him by brute force would have taken a severe toll of his strength.

"One three times a day," Charlie instructed, handing over the tablets which Kenneth had prescribed. "And keep him quiet. Mr. Carr will call tomorrow." She stroked Tim's head. He had stopped yowling and his poor frenzied eyes had closed dreamily against the light from his own garden. He let her touch him, he even managed to communicate that he did not find it disagreeable. Status had changed. Enemy she might still be, but she was defeated.

Tim Roberts had won home.

Miss Roberts had got out the coffee cups. She would not hear of Charlie leaving without some. There were twenty minutes before surgery began at eleven and it seemed a good opportunity to discuss Tim's after-care. His owner's gratitude was humbling. In practice, Charlie had done very little, not a quarter of what she would have liked.

It was eleven when she succeeded in getting away from Lime Tree Cottage and marginally later as she came to the gates into the yard. First arrivals would be waiting. But she would not keep them much longer. A minute would draw the bolts on the engraved glass door and whisk her behind the reception desk.

And goody, no one was standing outside.

She locked the car and hastened to the side entrance. It made her jump to realise that the main door had been opened and some clients were already sitting in reception. Nothing for it now but to face the music. She did so with her best smile.

"Good morning. Sorry for keeping you. I'll be with you in a minute."

There were five people waiting and most of them smiled back. Her eyes travelled to the end of the row and stopped. She saw thick blonde hair swirling into a curvy bob, dark glasses, a knotted rope of pearls, a grass green shirt.

Was she going mad? *It couldn't be* . . . But it was. The figure removed her glasses and waved them. "Don't mind me, dear. Go right ahead." Ruth Lavender said benignly.

The whole room was interested. Charlie did not blame them, but it was embarrassing. "Is something wrong, Mummy?" she asked anxiously.

"Not one thing, honey," Ruth said happily. "The chance just came up and I took it. We can have lunch together, in that nice place with the moon outside."

"*Cheese*," Charlie corrected absently. She was non-plussed. Not that she wasn't glad to see her mother, but, to be truthful, not here. Mummy was a super person, but she was lethal to concentration.

Kenneth was in the surgery. "I'm terribly sorry," Charlie began. "Miss Roberts made coffee. I should have refused it."

"No harm done," he said accommodatingly. "Get your breath and stop looking as though something awful had happened."

"Something awful *has* happened," she confided, red-faced. "My mother is out there."

His jaw dropped. "Your mother? Out there?"

"In reception. She's come to take me to lunch."

"And that's something awful?" His brows had risen.

"No. No, of course it isn't." She was loathing herself for the mess she was making. "Mummy's a darling. But she—well, I can't make out why she's here."

"Then let's find out." He put his head round the jamb of the door and withdrew it. "The lady in green—looking like Bette Davis? I congratulate you, Charles. Please show her in."

The meeting went well.

Ruth came with a swing of pleated skirt and the smile that made an unclassic face lovely. Kenneth gave her a warm handshake and an invitation to lunch. "And now how can we amuse you till one o'clock?" he mused. "I wonder is Jasmine free?" His hand strayed to the telephone.

"No, please," Charlie said urgently. "Mummy can wait in the flat."

"But of course. No trouble on my account. Please," Ruth supported.

"A kindness." Kenneth assured them. "You can vouch for that, Charles. Jasmine gets very tired of her own company."

It ended as Charlie had known in her bones it would. Jasmine asked Ruth out to the Manor, Kenneth sketched her a road map and sent her on her way with a wave and his narrow-eyed smile.

"I didn't realise your mother was American," he commented on his return. "She's charming."

"I know." All at once Charlie felt liberated. Misgivings were swept away. "You must think me dreadful."

"Must I?" His eyes were kind but penetrating. "I don't. It could be I've been in the same boat."

The moment seemed somehow to go deep.

"It was just—I was late already—" Charlie stumbled. "And I thought in work hours . . ."

"Another thing you think," he said carelessly, "is that I'm an ogre. Now shall we, at last, have our first patient?"

Sometimes the most unexpected things turn out best. Yesterday it would have seemed fantasy to picture a lunch party with Kenneth as host and her mother and herself as guests. Today it was fact and Charlie enjoyed every minute.

The Chuckling Cheese dining-room with its silver candlesticks and amber cloths was delightful and the excellent bill of fare included poached chicken in asparagus sauce. Ruth, who insisted on referring to it as 'The Man in the Moon', was her vivacious self. In fact she spilled out in her usual disarming way the whole family history.

"You were going to say you wouldn't have guessed it from Charlie. It's true. My husband was very English. And my dear good mother-in-law was directly descended from Jane Austen! Mind you, I loved her. But she certainly was the dominant colour and she reared the baby. You ask Charlie about her gran."

"I already have. I heard her talking to her one night," Kenneth said straightfaced.

"And I guess you wondered what you'd got in the house!" Ruth had a gay sudden laugh.

It was the mixture as before. Charlie was always dumb and witless when her mother got into her scintillating stride. It occasioned no resentment, just a slight wistfulness, and she was quite prepared for Kenneth to join in the fun.

Surprisingly, however, it was on her that his gaze rested and she could almost feel the compassion behind it.

"It's becoming a mite clearer," he said gently.

Ruth had had a lovely time. "I just adore this Man in the Moon," she kept saying. Woodsgift had also thrilled her and Kenneth's suggestion that she should come down one weekend and see more of it had gone down very well.

"I think Jasmine Buck is a remarkably fortunate girl," she commented to Charlie when they were alone. "If I took her right the decision is up to her. Is that the impression you got, honey?"

"I don't think I was looking for an impression, Mum," Charlie said carefully. "But—yes, it could be."

"No, honey," her mother retorted comically. "*You*

68

wouldn't have been looking. But remember, self-interest can be a terrific thing."

Her dash to the Cotswolds today had ostensibly been on business, but since the contributor she was to see lived considerably nearer Oxfordshire Charlie was justifiably suspicious. She also knew that her mother could wheedle almost anything she had a mind to, so extra time and petrol would be child's play.

"Now would I do such a thing?" Ruth disclaimed.

Charlie said : "Indubitably," and received a hug.

"I suppose I just got to thinking about you, honey. I'm happier now I've been here. That's a nice feller, even if he is spoken for."

Charlie started the next day on her own. Kenneth was vaccinating a flock of sheep on a farm some miles away. He expected to be back well before morning surgery, but around ten o'clock there was a phone call from another farm and a female voice reported a cow in trouble.

Charlie was sorry for the caller. Her husband had gone away for twenty-four hours and she was holding the fort. She had just discovered the casualty and thought it might already be too late. There seemed so little sign of life.

"I blame myself," she kept saying. "If my husband had been here he would have spotted it earlier. Have you any idea what I should do?" Charlie deduced, correctly as it turned out, that she was young and inexperienced, most probably a newlywed.

The trouble was she herself knew little in practice about large animals. One thing was sure—it would do no good to say so at this stage. She might not have been good with cows, but she *was* quite good with people.

"We'll soon find out," she promised briskly.

At the other farm it took a little time for Kenneth to come to the phone. As soon as she mentioned that the cow was down, felt cold and seemed unconscious he gave an exclamation.

"She had a calf on Sunday," Charlie added. She had assumed this must have something to do with it. It had. "Milk fever," Kenneth interposed. It rated emergency treatment. She could tell the farmer's wife that he was on his way and meantime the cow must be propped up. "That's so as the weight won't rest on her chest. If she's alive when I get there the rest is easy."

Charlie took up the scrap of paper on which she had jotted the number of the farm, and clicked her teeth in frustration. The telephone had rung.

"I wish to speak to Mr. Carr, please. Quickly," said an autocratic voice.

"I'm sorry," Charlie told it, "he's not here at the moment."

"Then kindly put me through to whatever number he left you," she was instructed.

In present circumstances that just was not possible. "Please hold the line," Charlie said firmly. Thank goodness the little switchboard had more than one line out. It enabled her to ring the cow's owner.

"Yes, I can manage that. I've got someone with me now," the latter said commendably. "Thank you very much. I'm grateful."

The other caller was not so satisfactory. "Hallo," she was saying impatiently when Charlie took the call back. "*Hallo*. Who is supposed to be attending this telephone?"

Charlie's cheeks reddened. "I'm very sorry. We had an emergency just then. Mr. Carr is on his way to it."

"Then intercept him," the voice commanded. "Young woman," it went on as Charlie was silent, "I presume you understand English."

Charlie drew a breath. "Mr. Carr will be on the road. I can't reach him for the moment. And I'm sure you'll understand, it's urgent. The cow he has gone to see may well be dying."

"Well, I want him at Mambury Towers," the caller stated. "Is that clear? Lady Turpin's cat has had a heart attack."

Charlie glanced at her watch. The time was approaching ten-thirty and it was highly unlikely that Lady Turpin did not possess a car.

"The best thing," she said in a conciliatory tone, "would be to bring it to the surgery. Mr. Carr will be here at eleven."

"Be so good, miss, as to spare me your opinion. I think I have a better claim on his time than every Tom, Dick

70

and Harry in the village. Will you kindly phone him wherever this cow is and pass on the message. And your name, please. What is it?"

"My name is Charlotte Lavender," Charlie said quietly. "And please don't go. If this is an emergency it will be quicker to bring the cat here. I don't know how long it will take Mr. Carr to get to Mambury, he's in the opposite direction at present."

There was a gasp of anger. "That is not the point, Miss Lavender. Mambury is the point. Surely we are entitled to a little more consideration than some farmer and his wretched cow!"

"Oh, Gran," Charlie thought miserably as the phone clicked, "I've done it now!" Lady Turpin had sounded livid.

The episode was worrying if only because she must give Kenneth the facts. She was wiping the table in the surgery with disinfectant when she heard the car door slam. He was coming across the yard, his grey tweed jacket frisking in the breeze. A stethoscope peeped from his pocket. He had not seen her and for a second she studied him—strong walk, brilliant eyes, wind-tousled hair.

The cow, he informed her, was on her feet again. He had been in time to give her the calcium she needed. "What other calls?" he asked, taking up the pad.

"Lady Turpin's cat," Charlie said woodenly. "She's afraid it's had a heart attack—and I may have upset her. I'm sorry."

"Upset Lady Turpin?" His eyes had narrowed as she had feared they might. "How, for goodness' sake?"

Before Charlie could reply, a second car drove into the yard and stopped.

"She doesn't look very upset to me," Kenneth remarked in a relieved tone. The stout smiling figure whose right hand gripped a basket had raised her free hand in a wave.

Kenneth went to the side door and beckoned.

"Oh, thanks, Ken," said a warm voice. "I always said Tiggy would break my heart, I'm afraid now he may have broken his own. Poor Tiggy! Always the exhibitionist." Charlie, hovering in the background, received a smile.

Something didn't fit, but she was unutterably grateful.

The visit was enjoyable for everyone except Tiggy. He was a fine tabby, long-backed and glossy and, according to his owner, 'packed a punch of steel'. He was also no more than three years of age. Kenneth, looking at the young muscular body, considered a heart attack improbable and a few minutes later he laid down the stethoscope and said : "As I thought, his heart is as sound as a bell."

Lady Turpin had not seen the start of the attack. She had simply heard what she described as 'whoops and war cries and Tiggy knocking himself from step to step of the stairs'. He had come into the morning-room, shaking his head, and rolled over. "Unless of course he's been offered a part in a film," she suggested.

Kenneth did not think so. "Just hold him, Charlie," he commanded. "I'll take a look at his ears."

Tiggy disliked being touched by the human hand, but he had been betrayed. He was so overcome by the treachery of it that he had no heart to resist. But every time Kenneth stopped for a fresh swab or a change of lotion he rose pathetically, his little hind feet scrabbling on the table top, and put his forepaws on his mistress's shoulders. 'Take me away', his big eyes beseeched.

"Oh, what a big brave cat it is," she said jovially.

Tiggy had ear-mites. Kenneth did not blame him for going berserk; low down in the aural passages the irritation could well produce dementia. He gave Lady Turpin a small plastic syringe and a bottle of lotion and sent her on her way. As she fastened the basket she enquired after 'the family', remarked that she had seen Jason last Sunday and he was getting as big as a house and reminded Kenneth of the church fête next Saturday.

"Not for me, I fear," he replied firmly.

He did ask : "What made you think you'd offended?" as the Mambury station wagon turned out of the yard, but with the waiting-room already crowded Charlie knew he was not anxious for a full explanation. In any case she could not have given one. Lady Turpin on the telephone and Lady Turpin 'live' had not seemed the same person.

"Thank goodness," she thought, and went to wipe down the table.

The vixen had no intention of dying, either from shock

or septicaemia. Her wound was healing and she devoured her rations of rabbit and sometimes chicken giblets with great greed. As her health improved so did her looks. She was a beautiful creature, but not to be trusted. Dropping her food into the cage still called for caution, Charlie had to be even more dexterous with the saucers of milk and water.

Old Martha had never returned. It was Charlie's private opinion that she had given her pet up for dead. Kenneth's intentions were as veiled. He was gratified by the patient's progress, but he had not altered his opinion of foxes in general.

"This fair lady mightn't attract you so much if you happened to be in the vicinity of a poultry run after she'd paid it a visit."

There was a happier prospect for Tim. Though he spent most of his time in the improvised pen—it was amusing to notice how his devoted mistress moved this about the garden from shade to sun—he had within forty-eight hours of his homecoming managed to lift his back legs over the rung of a table.

Not every day held episodes as dramatic as the vixen and the cow or as appealing as Tim; the emerging pattern was one of hard work. The small animal side of the practice had mushroomed in recent years and as it was in a rural area there was no shortage of the large animal work which had been the backbone of the business in Kenneth's grandfather's time. Kenneth himself worked long and tirelessly.

After the first two days no time was spared in chatting to his assistant and he made no further enquiries about Charlie's leisure time.

To date, this had been spent in exploring. It was from passing and repassing Lime Tree Cottage that she had observed the loving positioning of Tim's box.

Something more than halfway to Woodsgift a public footpath led to the village of Sedge. The evening Charlie followed it a couple of corncrakes called across the fields. It took her past a flock of geese on a green lawn. Nearer Sedge there was a rearing pen of pheasants, gorgeously gold and copper, and in Sedge itself a tiny church with a gilded steeple.

Another time she found a side road which went uphill under a vault of trees. A few minutes' walking and she realised where she was. These were the woods round Woodsgift, below her was Woodsgift Glen. On Sunday the walk she had taken with Kenneth and the children had come to this point.

True enough, there were the stone entrance piers into the back end of the woods. She penetrated a few yards and stood smelling the leaf mould and the bracken, her mind following the path on past the fox's lair to its green opening in the Manor garden. Ahead were the honey-coloured houses, Nicky the tearaway, Max the security guard, Jason and Samantha.

She must have stood for several minutes, lost even to the clop of hooves as a couple of schoolgirls on ponies went up the road above her. And then the sound registered. Was she mad, standing there practically trespassing? What would Kenneth think if he happened to come round the corner? What, Charlie asked herself, had *she* been thinking of?

The colour flamed through her cheeks and she ran stumblingly to the road.

CHAPTER FIVE

FRIDAY closed Charlie's first week in Hopehampton. Experience of Fridays in the London hospital had prepared her for a busy day, and it was all of that. The waiting-room was full long before eleven and Kenneth, who had been at a farm carrying out T.B. tests for the Ministry of Agriculture, was delayed. There were restive murmurs, two dogs snapped at each other and a toddler who had accompanied her mother took fright and started to cry. In the excitement a third dog fouled the mat. Kenneth came in to squealing dogs, a wailing child and the sight of his assistant shovel in hand.

Surgery ran late. A good samaritan brought in four stray kittens in the mistaken belief that 'a vet would always find homes for them'. She kept saying: "I was full sure you'd help," but she refused indignantly the humane offer which was made.

"I want to leave sharp on five," Kenneth announced before the door opened for the afternoon. He had been shopping. Parcels and a carrier bag were stacked in a corner. He had also had several phone calls which appeared to be personal.

It occurred to Charlie that he might be planning some relaxation after the busy week. Perhaps he was going out with Jasmine, or perhaps she was coming to dinner with him. It was a hot day with grilling sun. They had to draw the venetian blinds and she could not help thinking longingly of the greenwoods.

"What are you doing with yourself these days?" He shot the question unexpectedly as she was going out to man the reception desk.

She met it demurely. "Having a lovely time."

"Good. I trust you'll be supporting the fête tomorrow?"

Charlie had seen the posters and had received a handbill through her letter box. She had thought of looking in. "And you?" She remembered the conversation with Lady

Turpin.

"*Oh no*," he returned. "Not even for the motherland!"

Afternoon surgery also ran over, but by quarter past five the last patient had left and Charlie bolted the glass door. Kenneth was already outside putting his shopping into the estate car. When the phone rang and a frantic voice said: "Oh, please, this is an emergency," she wished she need not tell him.

Another cat was in trouble. Its owner thought it had been bitten by a dog, the wound was 'bleeding profusely'.

"All right, if she brings it now. Tell her I'll wait twenty minutes," Kenneth said resignedly.

It was nearer thirty before the caller arrived. The cat had a cut, quite small, on its shoulder. The bleeding had long since stopped.

Charlie experienced a rare moment of exasperation. Given a particle of common sense the casualty could have been treated at home.

"Are you not going to stitch it?" the cat's owner looked dubiously at the patch of fur Kenneth had clipped.

"I don't think it's necessary," he returned with commendable patience. "Just keep bathing it. I'll give him an injection. It doesn't look like a bite, just a bad cut."

This was not well received. The client bristled. "I'm sure it was a bite. There are new people next door to me with a terrier dog. It's a perfect nuisance—always in my garden. I intend to complain about it."

"Yes, well, that's another matter," Kenneth observed mildly. "I think this feller—" he scratched the cat's black head, "had a disagreement with barbed wire."

Charlie thought he had donated enough time. She brought the basket politely but pointedly: "Shall I give you a hand with him? I'll hold the lid open."

"That will be one-fifty," Kenneth remarked.

"One-fifty!" the client echoed. "You're very expensive, Mr. Carr." She made a half-hearted search of her handbag. "I haven't that much with me. Oh well, I suppose you'll send the bill."

"And so saying she walked out into the sunshine," Kenneth said softly as the door closed. "And all the trumpets sounded on the other side!" He clapped Charlie's shoulder. "As at this moment they're sounding for me! I must run."

Off to Jasmine, she thought, as he dived into the car. Oh well, he had earned his pleasure.

She sat longer than usual over her evening meal giving in to legs which had been on the go all week and allowing her eyes to dwell once again on the wall tile with its curious design. Just why was that horned creature standing on the chalice? She would have loved to know.

The teapot drained, she cleared away, hung up her long-sleeved uniform dress and put on a brief skirt and a deep blue cotton shirt. Where to go this time? The Common, she decided. It was the green cloth round whose edges Hopehampton, Sedge and other villages clustered, but so far her only encounter with it had been that incoming drive with Guy.

Many other people, it seemed, had had the same idea on this hot evening, but there was room for all. Hope-hampton Common had over six hundred acres.

Charlie stood for a few minutes sampling the expanse of open green. Cattle and ponies grazed, dogs frolicked, boys played cricket, cars skimmed along the roadways. The sense of space was invigorating. She walked quickly, shaking her head, feeling the breeze through her thick boyish hair.

Tom Long's post, she remembered, was where six roads met. It would tell her the way to go home. She went on, stopping to smile at a Dalmatian carrying a branch.

The white signpost was now in sight and at the same time she noticed a German Shepherd retrieving a ball. She had already watched the Dalmatian back to its mistress, the German Shepherd was going back to a... Charlie's jaw dropped. A man in a Shetland sweater, the colour of cornflakes, and a blue and white push-chair with a child in it.

Push-chairs would normally be part of the early scene with mothers. The little boy occupying this one had no mother. He was tucked snugly into a dark blue one-piece track suit and he was looking about him full of interest. His father, on the other hand, looked distrait. It was a shock to think of him as an ordinary mortal who could feel depressed.

He had seen her now and raised an arm in greeting. She went over, arriving at the same time as Max.

After the greeting Kenneth volunteered that Jason had had a cold but seemed over it now, so he had wrapped him up and brought him out for air. He then wiped the ball on the grass and handed it to Charlie.

"How are your overs? This dog plays as diligently as he works."

It was an amusing interlude. Charlie threw and Max bounded and skidded like a puppy. Evidently he functioned like a 'Seeing Eye' dog; when he was watching Jason in the garden he never let up, when it was playtime he made the most of it.

She paused once to re-roll the sleeve of her shirt and found Kenneth looking at her. "Why don't you wear that to work? It's most becoming."

"This old thing?" She could not credit her ears.

"It matches your eyes," he said gravely. "They really are like gentians."

"Thank you." Compliments were always a bit embarrassing, perhaps because she had not received that many. It was time to change the subject. Where was Samantha?

Samantha, she was informed, was having a night off. The school she attended was performing its end of term play. Sam had a leading role, she was a programme seller.

"It's been quite a day with him under the weather and her having to be lifted to Stroud. But that's how heroes are made. Observe the species, Charles. Like the prune, it's always full of wrinkles.

Charlie had been trained not to push herself. Her grandmother had a word for those who did. It was 'hussy'. Today, somehow, it seemed out of date.

"Why didn't you tell me?" she asked boldly. "I could have sat with Jason or taken Samantha to school. I'd have loved to." Loneliness could be a very practical thing, no one to go to the shops, no one to get a little girl ready for a social occasion, no one to decide when a little boy was well enough to go out. "Kenneth," it was the first time she'd got her tongue round it, "*will* you ask—any time? Please."

His eyes were nearly as blue as her own—but older. About eight years by the calendar, centuries in experience. She read this in the way they were looking at her. *He's kind, he doesn't want to hurt me, but he thinks . . :*

Oh, Gran, what is he thinking? Why did I say that? The colour rushed to her cheeks.

"That's very kind of you," Kenneth said gently. "But I'm beholden to so many good people as it is that I try not to add to the list."

"We'll walk along, then, shall we?" he added. "What way do you go?"

Charlie had to consult Tom Long's Post.

"You look as though you were choosing next year's holiday," Kenneth teased. "Let Tom Long take you to sunny Pin Farthings!"

In the end she settled unadventurously for 'Sedge— one mile'.

"Who was Tom Long? Do you know?"

"I don't think anyone does for certain. Some will tell you he was a notorious highwayman, others that he was a suicide. As I'm sure you know, such poor souls were always buried at crossroads."

He gave Charlie an opening to say that she knew very little about rural history and to find out, not unexpectedly, that Hopehampton was a treasure chest and she could have had no better hand to open it.

Out came the horse-drawn fire engine and the Fire Brigade commandeering any horses grazing on the Common to pull it in the event of fire. Out came the twice yearly fair with its dancing bear, fat geese and hobbyhorses. The carter trading in smuggled tobacco from sailors in London trundled up Tobacconist's Road and as a *pièce de résistance* the Long Stone in the fields south of the town girded up its loins on Midsummer Eve and went for a walk.

"Have you always lived here?" Charlie asked.

"In spirit," he answered briefly. "Not in flesh."

The practice had been started by his great-grandfather, but had skipped a generation because Kenneth's father, nineteen at the outbreak of the Second World War, had not had a chance to qualify. He had served in a tank regiment for seven years and with demobilisation a month away had been killed in a road accident in the autumn of 1946. At that time his young wife had been living in London with Kenneth, who was eighteen months old, but on pressure from the grandparents she had joined them in Hopehampton.

"She went for my sake," Kenneth said reflectively. "And I was as happy as a king. I put my roots down that first day and when I had to go away I left them behind me. They used to tug at my entrails from a world away."

"Where were you?"

"Australia. My mother remarried in 1957. My stepfather had come over here on holiday and he took us back with him to Sydney. This time it was the spiral in reverse. My mother had never been so happy, I was miserable. But promises had been made me and they were kept. As soon as my schooling was over Grandfather took me back. I got a place at Bristol, qualified, and the rest you know."

Many gaps remained and Charlie despised herself for her curiosity. She must not expect to hear about his marriage. Obviously it would open old wounds. "Miss Roberts praised your grandfather to me," she said gently. "I take it he's dead now?"

"Yes, for several years. My grandmother is still alive, though. She's living in Yorkshire now with her sister. And my mother is alive—and kicking! Hopehampton was never her element. She likes a faster pace—and an audience. As I somehow think *your* mother does. True?"

"How true!" Charlie laughed. "I'm far too quiet for Mummy. Sometimes she looks at me and I can hear her thinking : 'Where did I get her from?' "

In the present context it was almost a joke. She seemed to be looking back over her shoulder at the little mouse whose real self only the patients had seen. She did not feel mouselike now but totally extrovert.

She did not deserve the compassion that had suffused Kenneth's eyes.

It had been a short mile, covered twice as quickly as those in her own company. The green sea of Common had washed them up in Sedge. It was a quiet place and it had that rather un-English church with the gold leaf steeple and belfry. Kenneth asked if she had discovered it yet and suggested that it was worth a visit.

Max was given two commands: 'Sit' and 'Stay'. Jason, by this time nodding, blinked and was wheeled inside.

"He was christened here. Practically howled the place down," his father observed.

"And Samantha?"

"As far as I remember she was good. It was a long time ago. We put on a show for Samantha, in Hopehampton. My wife was like that."

Charlie's heart ticked over a mite faster. She could imagine what a happy time it had been. Two well-known families celebrating the first grandchild.

"I'm sorry," she said awkwardly. "One doesn't expect . . . it was very sad."

Again their eyes met, hers limpid with sympathy, his shuttered.

"Yes," he snapped it off so sharply that there was a pause. "In any case this church wasn't built then. So—what do you think of it?"

She thought very well of the church. It was small but brightened by white walls and plain windows, the one piece of stained glass a circle containing a dove. Against this austerity focal points stood out boldly—yellow gold reredos and altar covers, brass cross and candlesticks, an aumbrey ornamented in white and dark blue, a wrought iron crucifix on the plain white wall.

"You're interested in this sort of thing?" Kenneth had been watching her as she moved from one to the other.

"Yes, I love . . ." She stopped, finding it hard to explain. "I think it's the collector in me. I rather tend to collect places—this region particularly. I thought from the train it was like a picture book. More so than any other I've been to."

She was knocked off balance by the intense gravity of his stare. It made her face warm. And her heart. She had put it all very badly, but he seemed interested.

"How many do they number?" he asked gently.

The count was pathetically low because Gran's tastes had been repetitive. Strangely Kenneth's score was not much higher except for some winter sports holidays.

"Italy," he said suddenly. "I'd love to go to Italy and

81

to have all the time in the world. I'd go out of season and stay where the fancy took me. Rome, of course, and Naples, but not for too long. I'd soak up Venice and Verona, and linger in Florence—it's a beautiful town in the spring. I'd find a fairy godmother to come here and take over, then I'd throw a bag in the car and head for the romantics. What would you say to that, Charles? In modern repugnance, does it grab?"

The mood was infectious. Kenneth had seemed young on Sunday, but not in quite this sense. She answered him eagerly. "*Grab?* It *clamps*. Italy is a must for me too, someday."

"I think you'll have to come with me," he said lightly. "We'll make it a joint collection."

"Done!" Charlie joked. "Provided you take me to Assisi! For obvious reasons." No vet, she thought, should bypass St. Francis.

Kenneth took the point—or did he? His blue eyes rolled mischievously: "I'll take you to Assisi, let's not make it too obvious!"

As they were laughing footsteps fell in the aisle.

"What-ho!" a voice said caressingly. Jasmine was standing at one of the beechwood pews. She came forward fluidly. The sunshine of the past few days had turned her face dark gold. Against it her teeth were dazzling.

"Thanks for the signal, Ken," she added. "I've been looking for you all over."

"Signal?" Keneth's brows knit.

"Satellite, if that makes better sense." Bent over the push-chair, she made a nice angle in creased trousers and shoe heels. "He's waiting outside with his ears cocked. Would anything induce Nicky to do that?"

"Training would," Kenneth said briefly. "How is he?"

"Your mother-in-law says he killed one of her doves. She found its feathers this morning and descended on me. That's why I've been looking for you. Trust the old witch to come up with something the moment she gets home."

"Shall we go outside?" Kenneth suggested abruptly.

"Oh dear," Jasmine's voice retained its caressing note. "I've interrupted. You were lending her your shoulder and I've spoiled it. Mouse, my darling, sorry for butting in. I wouldn't have for the world. Your mother explained."

"My mother . . ." Charlie faltered. She was at a loss but apprehensive.

"There are times, Jasmine, when I marvel at your capacity for not making sense," Kenneth cut in good-naturedly. "For what purpose should I lend Charles my shoulder? *To cry on*?"

Jasmine flashed a hand to her face. "My motto is when you boob make it a big one. I can see I've spoken out of turn. I was thinking of Don, the silly guy who didn't know what was good for him."

"D-D . . . Don!" The name stuck miserably in Charlie's throat. It was at once unbelievable and only too horribly credible. In her impulsive extrovert way her mother must have talked about Don, and almost certainly had made it sound a far bigger thing than it had ever been.

"Your mother would like to take that boy apart," Jasmine remarked in a tone of saccharine. "She's very concerned about you. That's why she came down."

"She came because she had a job to do," Charlie struck

"And I doubt if there's cause for concern," Kenneth followed her smoothly. "I think the patient will live." For all that his glance was keen.

"Yes, I think she will too." Jasmine's glance was equally so. "You do at twenty-one. And there are always plenty more fish in the sea."

"In Hopehampton?" Kenneth looked amused.

Why in heaven's name, Charlie questioned, was he prolonging the conversation? He should have found it excessively trivial.

"Well," Jasmine said teasingly, "there was one quite nice fish biting within minutes, wasn't there? Now there seems to be a rival not a hundred miles away."

A thundercloud had gathered on Kenneth's brow. She saw it and backed.

"It's all right, I'm not serious."

"I should hope not," he said decisively.

Charlie was beginning to think that although the discussion was about her she might as well not be present. "I don't know what Mummy said, but it seems to have got in.

greatly out of proportion. Don and I were never more than friends. We still are."

"Well, shall we walk along?" To her embarrassed ears Kenneth's voice sounded bored. "It's getting late."

"I'll take that." Jasmine possessed herself of the pushchair. "And do listen, Ken," she commanded. "I cannot keep that dog. I had a card from his mistress, they still won't give her a date for her discharge. Anyway, she won't be fit to look after him. Far kinder to put him down."

"Oh no!" Villain though he might be, Charlie found the little beagle endearing. Could you blame him if his elderly owner had had no idea of training?

Perhaps not, but she could glean no encouragement from Kenneth's set face. "I suppose it could come to that," he conceded. "I hadn't really considered it in the long term."

The junction with the road leading back to Hopehampton was welcome. Charlie took it thankfully. To the right a gate with a chain on it led down into the woods. Kenneth took back control of the push-chair. Jasmine unwound the chain and opened the gate. Together they went down the path with Max bringing up the rear.

CHAPTER SIX

ON Saturday morning there were two familiar faces in the waiting-room. Stephanie Wychwood had brought Bobby for a booster injection. Since it was the day of the fête, virtually the entire village was over at the ground making ready and so far as morning surgery was concerned Kenneth might almost have closed his doors.

Charlie took advantage of the fact to make friends with Bobby. He was a nice little square shape, rather like a teddybear, the kind you instinctively cuddled. It was hard to believe such an innocent face could snap.

"You ask your boss!" Stephanie said feelingly. "It's only nerves, of course. He's not wicked. But it's embarrassing."

As it happened Bobby behaved well.

"You must have a soothing effect," Stephanie commended as Charlie relaxed her hold on the patient.

"The thought *has* occurred to me," Kenneth threw in unexpectedly.

Since Bobby had had some digestive upsets recently, he was also running the rule over him. Happily the verdict was satisfactory. Some powders were dispensed and the patient was free to go.

"Would you like to come up for coffee?" Charlie invited. "I'll hear the bell if anyone comes."

It was Stephanie's first visit to the flat and she was impressed. "He really has got the period to perfection, hasn't he? Anything too modern would be wrong with the courtyard and the archways. Oh, he's hung that, has he?" She was looking with obvious gratification at the title with the curious picture. "Good for him."

"You know where it came from?" Charlie asked curiously.

"I should do. It came from me," Stephanie admitted with a chuckle. "Jean, my sister-in-law, gives a party at Christmas and everyone takes along some little thing for a prize. That was my contribution. I found it in a funny little shop in Tetbury. Kenneth won it for trimming a hat! It was a marvellous hat," she added as Charlie's mouth fell open. "As far as I remember it had holly and mistletoe on the brim and an icicle from the Christmas tree on top. Quite a bold design. Original."

Perhaps that was where Samantha got her taste for headgear.

"I suppose you don't happen to know what it is? It's been intriguing me all week," Charlie submitted.

"Of course. It's a unicorn."

"It's standing on a chalice," Charlie observed.

"A cup," her informant agreed. "Kenneth was so interested that we ended up researching the subject and comparing our findings. Apparently it was believed that a unicorn, by dipping its horn into a liquid, could detect whether or not it contained poison. The Emperor Rudolf II—I think it was—had this design on his gold and silver plate. And we were quite thrilled about *our* horn." She pointed out the feature on the tile with a laugh. "You see it's parti-coloured. Now that's much older and more authentic than the popular conception of a white horn. Oh, but that's enough. I'm taking up your time."

"Oh, but I'm fascinated," Charlie said with truth. "What nationality were unicorns?"

"Greek or Roman. We were fascinated too after we read them up. They were thought to be quite small, actually about the size of a kid."

"Gracious!" Charlie had always imagined a unicorn to be like a horse.

"Not at all," Stephanie said firmly. She went on to explain that they were very swift creatures and so fierce that no hunter could capture them except by a trick. If you brought a young girl—but it had to be a virgin, she added, twinkling—and left her at the appointed place the unicorn would sense her purity and come and lay its head in her lap. "Quite charming," she concluded. "And of course much in the tradition of Greek mythology, where beasts played such an important part. Anyhow, I've kept my eyes open for a tile of the unicorn with a girl—the man in Tetbury remembers seeing some around—but no luck,

I'm afraid, so far. And now I must go. The dog hasn't had his dinner.

"You're coming to the fête, of course?" she reminded Charlie at the door. "I'll look out for you. I expect I'll have Samantha with me. Ken's very naughty about the fête, he never will go."

"Do you blame me?" a voice demanded roundly from the hallway where her nephew by marriage was standing. "These things place me between the devil and the deep blue sea. Either it's Sam wanting me to put my hand in my pocket for icecream or tatty comics or—what was it last time—*woollen hats,* or it's the whole parish wanting to talk about their sick animals."

"Most uncharitable, to say nothing of the swelled head," Stephanie commented. "After that I don't think I *will* compliment you on the flat."

Kenneth's unrepentant grin included Charlie in its scope. "You like it? Good. Now you find me the match for that unicorn and then we'll talk about my parochial duties." He saw Stephanie open her handbag and firmly closed it for her. "My pleasure. For Pete's sake, Steph, think what I owe you."

Altogether a pleasant interlude and one which Charlie found had put her right into the mood to enjoy the afternoon's festivities.

Business was booming when she arrived at the fête. Inside the entrance she was besieged by small sellers of raffle tickets. There was a queue for pony rides and another for icecream. A crowd had gathered round the clock golf. Unexpected but cheerful was the local talent accordion band playing on the lawn.

Also unexpected but heartwarming was the fact that she was recognised. Sometimes she could not put a name to the faces that smiled at her, though she knew they had been in the surgery during the week. Miss Roberts, naturally, was already a friend. She pressed Charlie to drop in any evening and rustled a bag of fudge invitingly under her nose.

A chunk was still wedged in Charlie's cheek when from behind someone clapped their hands over her eyes. The hands belonged to Guy. When she protested he transferred them amiably to her waist and walked her away with an arm about her to the novelty Dog Show where Lady Turpin was to decide on the dog she would like to take home.

"This is one way to get yourself talked about," Charlie murmured. She liked Hopehampton's young curate, but his gallantry was probably being misconstrued by about seventy per cent of his congregation.

"I know a better one," he returned, and lowered his head. Before she realised his intention a kiss dropped lightly on her cheek.

Charlie kept walking. She was staggered, even a little shocked. A kiss was one thing. It was quite another in the present context.

"I'd rather you hadn't done that," she said quietly.

"I'd like to change your mind, if I may," he murmured *sotto voce*.

"No—please," she said, troubled. All the anguish over Don seemed to be flooding back. If at that moment she was to see him walking across the lawn who knew how she would react. She had forced herself to be clear-sighted, but she was still emotionally involved.

Happily it was no time to try and be private.

"Gu-uy! Charl-ee!" yelled a childish voice. "Over here!" Samantha was standing across from them waving wildly.

She looked better than Charlie had ever seen her. The wretched bows were still cluttering up her hair, but she was wearing a pink dress patterned in flowery stripes and smocked to the waist. Jason was with her. He was bobbing up and down with excitement, dungarees of navy and yellow tartan making him amazingly tall. Both children gave Guy a rapturous greeting and Samantha demanded that he should come and watch her take Bobby into the show ring. He looked back ruefully at Charlie as they dragged him away.

Stephanie, however, soon came to claim her. "For goodness' sake look at these *killing* dogs! They're a scream!"

Lady Turpin at that moment was standing in front of a tiny dachshund which had decided to lie down but had kept its tail aloft like a rudder.

"She'll choose him, he's marvellous," Stephanie prophesied.

Lady Turpin, however, chose Bobby, who had laughed up at her from the end of Samantha's leash. It was a great occasion and Charlie was warmed by her own kindly welcome.

"Very nice to see you," the fête's patron beamed. "Have you been round the stalls? No? Then you should do that quickly before they get sold out. There are some lovely things."

"We haven't looked yet." Stephanie confided to Charlie. "It's a bit hard with the dog—he gets walked on. But you go. We'll have tea when you come back."

Charlie did not think it would take long to digest the contents of the half dozen booths which had been set up in a corner of the grounds. She made a few purchases of grocery goods and was within an ace of returning to Stephanie when something made her turn to the 'Antiques and Curios'. Next minute it was all she could do not to cry out. Someone was picking through a basket which had been labelled 'Wall Plaques'. She had a flower tile in one hand and in the other—suddenly Charlie felt weak with excitement.

"Don't take it, *put it down*," she willed silently.

It was a picture tile of a young girl. She was sitting on a bank and a strange little creature was laying its pointed horn in her lap.

"I don't know. The colouring isn't as pretty." The would-be purchaser was still hesitating. Finally—it was a breathless moment—she laid down the unicorn.

In the next second Charlie had grabbed it. She was waiting to pay the stallholder when Jasmine sauntered up. "Hallo, mouse, you're looking very pleased with yourself. What goes?"

"This." Charlie said proudly, and displayed the tile.

Jasmines's eyes scanned it disdainfully. "And this speaks to you, does it?" Clearly she did not think much of the find.

"Yes, but it will speak louder to Kenneth," Charlie laughed.

"Kenneth?" Jasmine echoed sharply.

Charlie dipped in her shoulder bag. "It's incredible," she said happily. "I only heard about this today. Miss

Wychwood has been trying for months to find one for him." Still fumbling for her purse, she added the necessary explanation.

Jasmine listened. She was, as always, in trousers, a brilliant cerise. The colour was picked up in her abstract patterned shirt and she had topped the lot with a short-sleeved white smock. It was a bold hard combination that made Charlie's dress look exactly what it was, the white with the turquoise stripes from the chain store. But there was no use worrying. Even if she had the wherewithal, she couldn't buy the other things that went to make the effect —aquiline features, midnight eyes, raven hair.

And fair was fair. She could be misjudging Jasmine. It had been civil of her to initiate the conversation. "She needn't have done that," Charlie admitted to herself. "I hadn't seen her."

By now she had located her money and turned back to pay for the tile. She had moved it prudently out of range, it was under her elbow. Or was it? For an instant her brow clouded, then cleared. Jasmine had picked up the trophy and was studying it.

"Interesting, isn't it?" Charlie remarked, putting out her hand.

Jasmine ignored the gesture. "Very," she said coolly, and waved the tile over her head. "Heigh up there, service!" she called to the stallholder. "I'm taking this."

It had to be a joke. But it wasn't—and it took only seconds to realise the fact.

"A bird in the hand, mouse," Jasmine said lightly.

"But I . . ." Charlie went hot and cold. It was so unexpected and so unfair.

"Don't look so fraught. He'll get it," Jasmine teased. "If he makes it worth my while." She flicked her fingers. "Hi, Betty! Can you take this from me?"

Maybe she *was* going to give it to Kenneth. Maybe that should have been all that mattered. It was not. Something primitive and alien took Charlie over.

"That's mine," she said loudly and firmly. "I had it first."

The heads, now turning curiously, would normally have shocked her into submission, but today they didn't. As

Jasmine drawled: "Too bad, mouse, it's mine now!" she stretched upwards and snatched. It was undignified, but it was also the last thing Jasmine had expected. Charlie was tall, she was slender and short skirts made her look a mere child, but she had the height when she cared to make use of it.

"Sorry," she said pantingly as the other's grip loosened. "I'm sure you can find something else."

Jasmine appeared to be speechless, speechless but very angry. Pinpoints of fury sparked in her eyes. She made no attempt to find a second tile, but turned and walked quickly from the stall.

The incident took away much of Charlie's joy, but not all. She had her pictured unicorn. It had been almost as dearly won as the animal itself.

"Well, I never!" Stephanie said, staring. "Talk about beginner's luck! I can hardly believe it. Don't take your eyes off it. It might vanish!"

She little knew, Charlie thought sheepishly. Anyway, another point had to be settled. Jasmine had stooped to trickery, but Stephanie was a different matter. "It was you found out about it in the first place," she said fairly. "I'll let you have it if you like."

"Good gracious, I wouldn't dream of it," the older woman declared. "It's yours, dear. I'd just like to see Ken's face when he sees it."

He would be delighted, Charlie thought glowingly. He would be astonished too, he would probably open his eyes wide and stare. The beauty of it was that it was such an opportune gift and so perfectly permissible—almost a joke. No eyebrows could possibly be raised at her giving him that particular present.

And he deserved the pleasure, small as it might be. One thing the week had shown her was that he had scant, if any, time to think of himself.

The fête went merrily ahead. Guy brought the children back from the pony rides but declined regretfully to join the party for tea. Stephanie said mischievously that he had to 'spread his favours'. The band played *Country Gardens*, Samantha chattered happily and Jason joined in. Last night in the push-chair he had seemed remote and small. Today he was a little boy running sturdily over the grass.

Charlie admired Samantha's dress and Stephanie gave a chuckle. Again she had been the provider. "Praise it as much as you like," she whispered. "Samantha doesn't care for it. I was hoping someone would tell her how nice she looked!"

Stephanie could be described as the salt of the earth. She was humorous, unsentimental and seemed to be constantly engaged on works of mercy. It was a shame about the dress. It was so pretty. What had gone wrong?

"It's not a maxi," Stephanie whispered back. "Samantha is very 'with it'. I'm not. Oh, she was most polite—she's her father's daughter. But I knew. Actually I was very sorry."

It was a pointer to where the speaker, good as she was, might fail. Stephanie was happy not to be a fashion hound, but what about Samantha? It also threw a new light on Kenneth's daughter, now plying Jason with the last of his buttered scone.

"That's for Daddy and that's for Max, and who's this for?"

Jason shouted something unintelligible and was reproved. "Oh no, Jay, that's not nice. We *never* speak with our mouth full."

Sadly, it was apparent that Jason liked his own way. "It's for witch," he yelled, so loudly that there was no mistaking the words. "Witch, witch, witch! Where's the old witch?"

As the sound died away you could have cut the silence. Samantha's face had frozen. She was staring as though transfixed at Charlie's side of the table. By contrast Jason was delighted. His beam was seraphic. " 'Lo, witch!" he piped.

Charlie swung round to see a slim middle-aged woman. She had a frail face, small dark eyes and a mouth that looked as though it was tasting lemon.

"All right, Samantha," she said coldly. "I know you call me that behind my back."

"Oh no." Samantha was a bad liar, but she did her best. "No, Granny, truly we don't."

Granny! So this was Jean Wychwood. Charlie's impression was two-fold—the newcomer's elegance and

Samantha's look of horror. She heard confusedly Stephanie's voice: "Have you had tea, Jean, or will you join us? You haven't met Charlie yet," and rose.

The eyes like dark gimlets seemed to be boring into her own. "In a sense we have met," Jean Wychwood said icily. "At least, we have spoken. I'm sure Miss Lavender will recall it. I telephoned on behalf of my friend, Lady Turpin."

Help! *It had been Jean Wychwood.* Charlie had been only too happy to forget the mystery voice which had caused her such trepidation. Nothing could possibly have prepared her for the identity of its owner, though it was true that yesterday Jasmine had complained about Ken's mother-in-law stirring up trouble from the moment she arrived home.

"Yes. I'm sorry about that," she said quietly, and held out her hand. "I know how anxious you were about Tiggy. Thank goodness it was not as bad as it looked. And you'll be glad to know Mr. Carr got to the cow in time."

Stephanie, knowing nothing of the incident, must have read the discomfiture in her face. "No talking shop!" she decreed. "We're here to enjoy ourselves." In seconds everything was under control. Samantha was directed to the next table where there was an unoccupied chair. "I'm sure you could bring that over for Granny," and somewhat regally Jean Wychwood accepted it.

She was a stylish figure, more in keeping with royal Ascot than a village fête. Pearls were in again and worn with a high-waisted pale beige coat. Stockings were white, the square-toed brown shoes matched the brown leather handbag. There was a cloche hat, ghost beige with ruchings of satin. But somehow her presence put a damper on the proceedings. Samantha lost her tongue and Jason took pattern by her and kept quiet. It was left to Stephanie to keep the conversation going, but, able as she was, no one could call it a cheerful gathering.

"Don't take too much notice of Jean," Stephanie managed to whisper as Charlie was leaving. "She's off-putting, I know, but she's her own worst enemy."

All in all, it had been a day of problems. Charlie broke them down tersely and bluntly.

Guy had to be gently discouraged, difficult because he was so nice but, in fairness to him, essential.

She had herself made an enemy of Jasmine, the last thing she wanted. It was horrible to be bad friends.

Jean Wychwood seemed unhappy and made others so.

Samantha was afraid of her grandmother and that was a tragedy.

Nicky the beagle might have to be put down and that would be double tragedy. His mistress would break her heart.

Why go on? The next pair on the doom list were old Martha and the vixen. It was some time since Kenneth had mentioned the latter, but one of these days Charlie knew the exercise would be completed and he would end its life.

One way and another the day had lost a lot of its gold. But there was one maxim in which her own dear grandmother had put great faith. 'Don't try to do tomorrow's work today.' She remembered it now and took the advice to heart.

CHAPTER SEVEN

NEXT morning she met Stephanie and Samantha at the church door.

"Sit with us, won't you?" Stephanie invited.

Charlie found Samantha enlivening company. She was obviously pleased to have an addition to the party and pointed out the sights of the church in a loud undertone. Her friend Brenda in the choir merited a particularly long whisper.

"Sam, you shouldn't talk, dear," Charlie cautioned. "Not in church."

She was unhappy about the instant way in which Samantha's face clouded. Perhaps when the child was already old beyond her years it would have been permissible to overlook the chatter.

A minute later Jasmine passed up the aisle. She took a pew which was otherwise empty and looked back to smile. It was a relief that yesterday's pique seemed to have abated. Under the big hat her face was beautiful again, her look caressing. When she patted the empty seat beside her and made a lonesome moue Samantha was not proof against it. She was into the aisle like a shot and over to join her.

It was such a small thing, and yet it rankled. A declaration of allegiance? A choice?

Well, why not, Charlie admonished herself sternly. Had she not realised immediately that Jasmine was a 'candle' person? Samantha was only following in her father's footsteps.

Outside once more in the sunny breezy churchyard Guy came up to speak to them. He looked hurtfully young, his fair hair streaking his forehead and his long cassock making him more like a rod than ever.

"Will you be over this afternoon?" he asked Charlie, and before she could say no Stephanie chimed in, "She will. She's coming to me this time. You may drop in too if you're good."

95

All in all, there was such a wave of bonhomie that when Jasmine emerged Charlie took the bull by the horns. "If you really want that tile," she said resolutely, "you can have it. I'll bring it this afternoon." Jasmine would give it to Kenneth, there was little doubt of that, and that afer all was the thing that mattered.

It was a trifle disconcerting to see the amusement in the dark eyes before her. "Well, there's a change!" their owner observed lightly. "What is it, mouse? An act of contrition? I did think Guy read that lesson rather beautifully."

"It's got nothing to do with Guy," Charlie said crossly. "Just that if you want it . . ."

"Not any more!" Jasmine chipped in gaily. "Keep it and make sure the price is right!"

Charlie, who wished fervently that she need not be called 'mouse', tried to stifle the irritation it produced. Jasmine, she told herself, had accepted the olive branch and been generous in her turn. It was good to know they were no longer on bad terms.

"Did you see Brenda in the choir?" Samantha was now asking Jasmine wistfully.

There was no doubt about the glamour which attached to a blue cassock. "Poor Sam," Charlie thought tenderly. "Why do we always want what we can't have?"

"Do you mean the little fat one with the red face?" Jasmine asked carelessly. "You're much nicer than that."

Samantha's face lit up. "Am I? Am I really?"

"But of course," Jasmine cooed. "You, my sweet, are an individual. And your voice is the greatest. Now are you coming home with me?"

Charlie's grandmother would not have approved of the tactics. 'There are some things in life we can't change, so we might as well get used to them,' was another of her favourite maxims. Charlie thought Samantha might as well face the fact that at the moment she did not sing in tune. Possibly something could be done for her, but that was a different matter.

It made her uneasy to see the light breaking over the child's face.

"Let's see if we can find an icecream shop open," Jasmine suggested, preparing to sweep Samantha away.

It seemed, however, that Stephanie had other ideas. "I think Samantha had better come with us," she stated flatly.

"And why should that be, I wonder? Don't you good people trust me?" Jasmine began.

"Surely it's simple," Stephanie returned placidly. "She's in my charge."

"Oh, come on!" Jasmine exploded. "This is too silly!" She dropped Samantha's hand and whipped across the grounds to the lych gate.

Charlie was sorry for Samantha, whose disappointment showed.

"The trouble with Jasmine is that you're never quite sure of her," Stephanie whispered. "She might just forget about Samantha if she met someone more interesting."

Jasmine's orange car had pulled away by the time they reached the road, but just as Stephanie was unlocking hers Samantha cried out: "Look, there's Daddy!" and pointed down the hill.

Kenneth in shirt-sleeves was walking towards them, Jason swinging out of his hand. He had a clean cool look about him, blue grey shirt, dark tie, short hair, and deeply ground suntan. Even Jason had the masculine touch. His minuscule shorts were putty colour, his top navy.

"Can anyone tell me," Kenneth asked them scornfully, "why my brother-in-law reserves his long sermons for the Sundays I'm in church and lets you out early when I'm not?"

Stephanie took up the challenge. "Yes, *clever*! He wasn't preaching today! Did you want Samantha? You nearly missed us."

"So I see." He included Charlie in the general smile. "Yes. Come on, Sam, work to be done. And Charles . . ."

The next words were drowned. A car's horn had sounded sharply. Jasmine's sporty orange was back, drawn up on the opposite side of the road. Jasmine herself leaned from the driver's window.

"Hi, Ken, I saw you walking. Want a lift?"

Kenneth looked startled. "Oh . . . no, thanks. I have the car. It's below."

Jasmine sauntered across. She pushed her large hat off

97

her forehead and looked as though she was trying not to smile. "As I see the two of you together, did you tell him, mouse, or shall I?"

Charlie shook her head. "I'm not with you." It sounded as untruthful as it was. She had a nasty feeling Jasmine was going to refer to the unicorn tile and the time and place were wrong.

"Has something happened?" Kenneth looked from one to the other.

"Indeed, darling. Yesterday," Jasmine told him in honeyed tones. "Battle of the year—over you."

"Oh, please!" Charlie began, scarlet-cheeked. "She's joking."

"You should have been in church, Ken," Jasmine went on, ignoring her. "It had a very salutary effect. Suddenly I felt sorry for my sins and so did she. I don't know what you do to us, you lucky man, but here's me, three years a camp follower, and poor Charlie not ten days yet and hooked."

"What are you talking about?" Kenneth demanded.

Charlie had no words. She stood mute and wretched wishing the ground would swallow her.

"We both wanted to buy you the same present," Jasmine confided sadly.

"Present? There's no need to buy me a present."

"Now isn't that ungrateful? You'll ruin it," Jasmine reproached. "*She's* going to give it to you—it's the spoils of victory."

"Will someone kindly explain?" Kenneth demanded.

"Yes, darling, I let her win," Jasmine answered. "Brave little me. I thought she was going to scratch my eyes out—no kidding. It's as bad as that, I do assure you."

Charlie knew it was ridiculous. Common sense told her that Jasmine was not achieving even her usual comedy effect. But common sense came a long way down the list. There was also a ghastly drift of truth, shaming, shattering, cruel. She could not bear one second more of Kenneth's crinkling gaze. Farewells be hanged—she just wanted to get away.

Mouse was Jasmine's mocking name for her. It was exactly how she felt as she put her head down and scurried across the road. 'Not ten days yet and hooked.' The phrase rang in her ears. Was that how it had seemed to the onlookers at the fête? Was that how it would seem to Stephanie? Appalling beyond words, was that how Kenneth would take it?

By this time feet were running after her.

"Charlie, wait!" Samantha called gaspingly. "Daddy wants you." Red bows a-flutter, she skidded to a stop.

Behind her came Kenneth and Jason at a slower pace. Jason was doing his best, but his legs were short. The sight of the anxious little face sent Charlie back to meet them.

"Yes? Did you want me?" she asked coolly.

"What does it look like?" Kenneth retorted. "You took off like a rocket."

"With reason."

"With no reason at all. Surely you can see a joke." His voice was cold.

"I *can*," Charlie flashed.

"Meaning this wasn't one? In that case I'm flattered."

"No, I don't mean that! You're twisting me."

"If you're not careful I shall be smacking you," Kenneth returned calmly. "Jasmine meant no harm."

"Rubbish!" Charlie said loudly, and subsided. She had forgotten herself—forgotten the staring children, forgotten that he was her employer and Jasmine the girl he admired. In short there was nothing that she had remembered. The realisation made her feel hot and cold. "I'm sorry, I forgot," she muttered.

"Forgot what?"

Samantha and Jason had moved away. The scene seemed to have narrowed to a pair of dark blue eyes, steady as stone and very, very perceptive.

"Who I was speaking to." Something pierced her consciousness. "To whom I was speaking," she amended.

"That's better." The eyes twinkled. "But don't remember too soon or too often, will you? You have a peculiar way of coming to life when you forget yourself. I find it intriguing. And may I say with all confidence your grandmother wouldn't have known you."

Charlie could not see how she looked, but she sensed

99

that her cheeks were blazing peach and this probably picked up the vivid honey amber lights in her hair. Her quivering anger was so unaccustomed that it affronted her.

"I'm glad you find me entertaining. It means I needn't apologise."

"Perhaps it's I who should do that," Kenneth said gently. "On Jasmine's behalf I do. She and her father are friends to whom I owe a great deal. I hope you'll find yourself able to accept her nonsense. It's an integral part of her and quite unmalicious."

Obviously the conversation had to be ended. "If you say so," Charlie concurred, and made to move away.

Just as obviously Kenneth understood that this was the most she could concede. "Right," he returned briskly. "Now, business. I want you on this call !"

An hour ago Charlie would not have hesitated. Where the patients were concerned she was at his service any time. Now there was that hairsbreadth of doubt. To consent without question might give the wrong impression.

"An emergency?" she murmured. "If not—well, it is Sunday morning."

"Captain Bligh to Fletcher Christian," Kenneth returned. "Is this a mutiny?" He was smiling and his eyes looked like lapis lazuli.

"You know it's not. I was just making clear . . ."

"That your feelings for me are not as Jasmine suggests. Superfluous Charles ! That's never been in doubt. But let me reiterate. That's not the purpose of the exercise. As to this morning, come if you like, it's all the same to me."

That fact was so fundamental it could hardly have accounted for the little cold pang she felt. "Of course I'll come. Do you want anything from the office?"

Kenneth had left the car ready. He packed the children into the back seat, told them not to touch anything and set off. The road branched off in the opposite direction to Sedge, Woodsgift and the Common. Soon it opened into green. "If you're interested in archaeology, there's a long barrow just after we turn off," Kenneth said seriously. She had the feeling he was laughing at her. She had only a vague notion what a 'barrow' was and he was always so effortlessly knowledgeable.

"The Long Stone is just opposite it. No doubt you'll be watching it walk on Monday week," he made a joking reference to the Midsummer Eve superstition.

It seemed to Charlie that this side of Hopehampton was altogether different from the other with its woods and houses and its glimpses of roses in gardens. This was wilder, with only one farm signposted and the mention of tumuli from the Bronze Age seemed quite in keeping. This was old England still ticking away in the quiet. She had a feeling about it.

'*The evil that men do lives after them*', she recalled. It could account for the sudden dread she had. This lonely stretch boded no good. On the other hand, it could be just fancy.

They drove on.

"In the fourteenth century all this was known as Great Field," Kenneth remarked. "We're just coming to the Devil's Churchyard."

Charlie sat up, not because there was anything gruesome about the round green hollow to which he had pointed, but because this surely was the place where old Martha had her shack. "You never said we were going to see Martha."

"You never asked." He had started to slow down.

"But why?"

"Oh, because there are some things she ought to be told. I've done with the vixen, Charles. I don't think I caused it much suffering."

"And you've come out to tell her?" Charlie's mouth felt dry. The end was not unexpected, but she supposed in her heart she had been hoping for something different.

"I thought one of us should tell her, yes," he said detachedly. "She appeared to be attached to it."

Charlie darted a glance into the back of the brake and met Samantha's popping eyes. Granted that whatever must be must be, it did seem an insensitive approach.

To the left of the picture a rough shack could now be seen. Smoke was coming out of its chimney and the puzzled dirty dog which had accompanied the party to the surgery a week ago was sniffing about at the door. Very deliberately Kenneth sounded the horn. "Why tell her?" Charlie rebelled inwardly. The memory of the seamed old face rose before her. "She knew. Why not leave it at that?"

"Daddy!" said Samantha sharply. "There's a basket on the floor in the back."

The silence was thick. Charlie turned her head.

"Did you expect it would sit on your knee?" Kenneth retorted.

The door of the hut had opened and a familiar figure had shuffled out.

"You mean—it's still alive?" Charlie stammered. *"You're giving it back to her?"*

"Not I," he corrected. "I wouldn't have that on my conscience. You know what I think of foxes." He met their faces blandly and a trifle distantly. "I repeat, as far as I'm concerned that one has ceased to exist." There was the faintest twinkle in his eye. It told her all she needed to know.

"Quickly, Sam, give me a hand," she said urgently, and opened the door.

Martha was a tough old bird. She did not weep easily or beautifully, nor, Charlie suspected, willingly, but the miracle had taken her unawares. As for the vixen, she nipped out of the cage and sat down in the sunshine beside the tousled old terrier. The strange little family was once again complete.

"You did a wonderful thing," Charlie told Kenneth as they drove home.

"Against my better judgement," he said stonily.

The expedition had delayed lunch. She had no sooner cleared away than it was time to get ready for Woodsgift. Stephanie's invitation had been for four o'clock, but Charlie had specially requested that they should not come in for her. She was slipping on a jacket when the door bell pealed.

"Hello," said Guy, ducking a little as he smiled. "Ready?"

For an ungrateful moment Charlie felt disappointment. She loved the way by Well Hill, knew the ponies that grazed in a field farther along and had once seen a pair of grey squirrels frolicking in the trees this side of the white gate to Woodsgift. The walk was always a pleasure. She hoped Guy had not come in specially.

He reassured her quickly. His mother had had a message for a friend in the town, so he had driven her in.

It was a little disconcerting to see Jean Wychwood's elegant coiffure through the car window. Yesterday's pretty cloche hat had hidden it; today silvery and curving round her small head, it was all of a piece with the pale smartly seamed coat. Guy's mother looked no more affable than she had been on the previous afternoon, but Charlie was at least given a pinched smile and a greeting. "Good afternoon, Miss Lavender. It's a little cooler today."

She took it as an olive branch. "Yes, quite a bit. Thank you for picking me up."

"No trouble," Jean Wychwood allowed. "We were passing."

It was not effusive but it was familiar. As a small child hurtling to meet her grandmother she had been unfailingly corrected for exuberance, as a bigger one airing schoolgirl exaggerations she had been pulled up for extravagance. She had never minded unduly, nor, with the legacy those days had left, had she ever had difficulty in communicating with the older generation. There were some debits about being 'an old-fashioned little thing', this was one of the credits.

"I expect you were pleased with the result of the fête?" she asked decorously. It had been announced in church that morning as a record.

She had made a wise choice of subject. Jean Wychwood had been actively engaged in the running of the fête and had actually masterminded the Antiques and Curios stall. Her normally frigid manner thawed considerably when Charlie praised the interesting display of tiles and wall plaques.

"Did you find any that took your fancy?"

"Oh yes. A unicorn." Not without an inward blush— her memories were still painful—Charlie described her purchase.

To her gratification Guy's mother became quite human. "I know the one you mean. As a matter of fact I was responsible for its being there." An old parishioner on whom she had called had given her permission to rummage in the attic. She had noticed the tile and had considered buying it herself. Then she had decided that would have been taking advantage. It was exactly the principle Charlie's grandmother would have followed.

"I must say, Miss Lavender, I'm glad you happened upon it, since you appear so interested," she concluded almost benignly. "I expect you know Jean Moreau's *Ladies and Unicorns*. I have a nice reproduction of it if you would care to see it."

Charlie accepted with a mild feeling of elation. She had been very anxious to wipe out their unfortunate first encounter and she would not have been feminine if the graceful white house had not on the instant filled her with a desire to see inside.

"I have the old dower house," Jean Wychwood informed her as they drew up. "I daresay you know that my late husband developed the estate into its present form. In the old days we lived in the Manor. Unfortunately it's too large for my altered circumstances. I suppose I must face the fact that Guy won't be in Hopehampton for ever."

Development, Charlie thought, must come easily to the Wychwoods. Apart from the masterpiece of the water garden, Jean's embellishments to the house were assured. There was a brass carriage lamp by the front door and the curving wall of the forecourt had an alcove containing a bust.

Inside, the drawing-room, a collector's paradise, was dominated by the unicorn painting. In the style of the French Romantics, the fabled creatures had been shown at play with young girls in a garden. Details like an eye, a nostril and the point of a horn gave them ferocity. Graceful and beautiful as they were, they were still fighting beasts. The champions and defenders of chastity, and untameable except by a pure maiden.

"I could stand and look at them all day," Charlie declared.

"Then you must certainly come again," Jean Wychwood returned. "We'll fix a day. It's a change to find someone who can appreciate good things."

"You made a hit," Guy said warmly as they walked on to Stephanie's house.

"I like your mother." She was able to reply quite truthfully. "As a matter of fact she reminds me of my grand-mother. I miss Gran very much. We were great friends."

"You don't know what a miracle it is," he continued naïvely. "You're the first girl-friend I've had who didn't wilt on sight! Mother doesn't exactly shine to them either. But she likes you, I can tell."

"Oh no!" Charlie thought frantically. Here it was again. Guy *couldn't* be falling for her. She would do anything not to hurt him, but he couldn't be encouraged to hope.

It was, however, no place for a serious discussion. Already Bobby had spotted them from his vantage point on the terrace and was alerting his mistress. Stephanie came hurrying out to greet them.

Charlie was beginning to feel that she had been in Hopehampton far longer than a week. The little colony in Woodsgift, after only three visits, seemed like a second home. From her hostess's sitting-room she could see Jean Wychwood's lake in its dell, the front of Kenneth's house with its array of rose bushes, and the path curving round behind it to the Manor. Stephanie must have read her thoughts, for suddenly she observed that it was a pity Kenneth's surgery was not attached to his house. "Then you'd be here all the time. Perhaps you wouldn't like that, of course!" Her glance was merry.

As Charlie started to say how much she would like it Guy cut in ruefully: "That's Mother's fault, of course. She put a spoke in that wheel."

Kenneth, he explained, had wanted just that. The lease of the buildings in which the practice had been conducted 'since time immemorial' had expired two or three years ago and he had tried to build new premises in the Manor grounds. Jasmine's father had been agreeable, but Jean Wychwood had lodged an objection.

"I don't think I'd have minded," Stephanie said fairly. "I thought about the drawbacks, but compared with what it would have meant to Ken I'd have gone along with it. He's a very good neighbour, you know, does all sorts of things for me. The help I give him with the children isn't at all one-sided. And then Marjorie had just died and he was at his wits' end, poor man. But in the end it all worked out very well."

"I was going to say I don't think you could improve on the present surgery," Charlie put in.

"Well, of course that was due to Mr. Buck, Jasmine's father," Stephanie told her. "He put up the money."

Charlie began to see what Kenneth had meant that morning when he had referred to the debt he owed Jasmine and her father. It seemed too that the strong business connection would be an added argument for Jasmine to put aside her prejudices and settle for a country life. There was so much to commend it—a house in this beautiful setting, two children who already loved her, her father near at hand and Kenneth.

The world seemed to go still when she thought of Kenneth. He had such presence and beneath it such compassion. He spoke with such care. How, for instance, would he frame a proposal?

Suddenly her cheeks flamed. She felt the warmth wriggling through her and, shamingly, Stephanie's enquiring glance.

"Do you find the room too warm, Charlie? You look hot."

"Time for some fresh air, perhaps," Guy suggested promptly. "You haven't seen Hannibal yet. Come and I'll introduce you."

It was a little presumptuous since he was not the host, but Stephanie interpreted Charlie's hesitation and nodded assent. "Of course. Off you go."

"I thought I'd never get you to myself," Guy announced disarmingly as soon as they were outside. Shepherding her towards the Manor path, he slipped an arm round her waist. Again she wished he wouldn't. True, there were no parishioners today to draw the wrong conclusions, but they were still walking in full view of Stephanie's sitting-room.

"Would you mind if I said something?"

He was not slow-witted. "Probably enormously. Remember I saw you first!"

"I'm not likely to forget that," she said feelingly. "Or how kind you were. But don't let's be serious, please. It wouldn't be fair."

Guy's nice thin face broke into a smile. "Let me worry about that. Just so long as I don't put you off?"

"Oh, never." Perhaps she was being too truthful for her own good. She thought so next instant when she found herself being squeezed. He had a sort of laughing chin and he looked gay and elegant in a black shirt and a gorse yellow sweater.

"A darling," she thought. "But I don't love him. Not like that. He makes me feel like a mother."

The path they were following topped Kenneth's garden. One of the charms of Woodsgift was its different levels. The drive climbed to the woods and steps led down from it to the Carr lawn and patio. The quiet had misled Charlie into thinking that nobody was at home, but in fact Samantha was lying on a rug with a book and Jason was raising a giddy tower of coloured bricks. Their father, alas, was kneeling on the top step of the flight weeding the bank.

His face was inscrutable, but he could not have failed to notice the squeeze or to hear the boyish chuckle Guy had given.

"I thought I was the only one who worked on Sundays," Guy observed.

"Is that what you call it?" his brother-in-law questioned drily.

"We're just going round to see Guy's horse," Charlie put in hastily. "And then I must be getting back."

"I'm sure there's nothing to hurry home for," Kenneth opined. "The weather's good and I can see the company is." He twinkled. "Why not make the most of it?"

It was apparent that the two men liked each other. Where a moment ago Guy had been all eagerness to display Hannibal, he now showed a disposition to linger. Somewhat embarrassingly he even went over their visit to his mother and how well it had gone.

"I'm delighted," Kenneth said cordially.

"I don't know what power this girl has," Guy went on, laughing, "but it worked wonders."

"No power was necessary." Charlie felt bound to strike a blow for the subject of the discussion. "Mrs. Wychwood was very kind and quite easy to talk to. Guy goes on as though I'd worked a miracle."

"If you didn't someone did," Jean Wychwood's son averred. "Honestly, Ken, you wouldn't believe it. I couldn't get a word in."

"A miracle in itself," his brother-in-law commented. "Now either take Charles away or allow her to take you. I've got work to do." He turned back smilingly to the task in hand.

"Did you hear that, Charlie? Something tells me we're being given a hint," Guy observed drolly. His arm went back to her waist and he piloted her on down the path.

Hannibal was an old horse and an old friend. He had belonged to Guy's father who, at one time, had been Master of the local Hunt. Hannibal's hunting days were over long since, but sometimes during the season Guy was in the habit of riding him over to watch the hunt because it gave him such pleasure to be near them. He was a docile horse and so used to the family at Woodsgift that he never needed the head-collar.

Now as Guy and Charlie approached the paddock they could see him watching them over the gate. He was a dark bay with a white race and not very big.

Guy presented Charlie to him and opened the gate. It was never necessary to lead Hannibal, he explained cheerfully; where other horses had to be held out to graze he would follow you. "'And mow the lawn on the way," he added. Plainly the old horse's evening excursion on to the greener pasture outside his own field was a little treat for them both.

She watched sympathetically as Guy went ahead. Hannibal was following just as prophesied when suddenly he began to cough.

"Hey, what's up?" Guy asked, turning back. He asked it lightly with obviously little apprehension.

Charlie could not claim a great knowledge of horses and their ailments, but she could see the "glub glub" catch of breath going all the way down Hannibal's neck. The sounds he was making were sadly easy to classify, as was the drawing back bracing movement.

"What is it, boy?" Guy was now deeply troubled. "Charlie, what it is? Do you know?"

"He's in pain." The horse had curled his lip back over his teeth as the spasm gripped him. "He's old, isn't he? I think he's having a heart attack."

At that moment the worst seemed to be over. A few minutes more and to all intents and purposes Hannibal was himself again. The rigidness left him and he even started to move.

"What should I do for him?" Guy asked. "It's bad, isn't it?"

Charlie had to admit that a heart attack was always serious, but she was anxious not to alarm.

"I think you should ask Ken to take a look at him. I could be wrong."

One thing was sure—the social part of the afternoon was over. Guy would have enough on his hands between now and Evensong. Charlie slipped back to make her excuses to Stephanie, who insisted on driving her home. It was a sombre finish to a day that had begun so happily.

"Poor Guy," Stephanie remarked. "I must admit I'm not very interested in horses, but my brother and his family were always very keen. Marjorie and Guy had ponies before they were five and Jean rode a lot when she was young. She's going to be upset about Hannibal, she'll feel it's another link giving way. Charlie, I do wish we could do something about Jean. I say this because Guy said she took to you. If she did, it's wonderful. She's so down on young people as a rule."

CHAPTER EIGHT

NEXT morning Charlie wrapped up the unicorn tile and took it downstairs to the office. As she did so the blue estate car drew into the yard. Kenneth got out and went to the tail gate. She saw him gather a leash into his hand. At the end of it, bouncing with excitement, was Nicky's stocky white form. Kenneth pulled on the leash and he jumped down.

"Come on, come on," Kenneth said tetchily.

His unsmiling demeanour was in contrast to the dog's. Nicky, as always, was in the best of form. His white paws twinkled across the cobbles, his tail was going like a flag, he was looking up adoringly.

Charlie opened the door and he fawned excitedly. "Is there something wrong with him?" she asked.

"Plenty," Kenneth returned shortly.

"I mean—is he a patient?"

"A detainee, unfortunately. Shut him up, will you? And for Pete's sake not where he can get loose." The tone was quelling.

"Yes, of course. I'll put him in a kennel," Charlie said uncertainly.

Something was amiss. She could only think that Hannibal had had another attack. Meantime, she had her orders. She secured Nicky and slapped him on his thick loin. "You're getting too fat." With an elderly mistress in poor health and Jasmine who could not be bothered about him this dog had never had a chance.

In the surgery Kenneth was scrutinising his message pad.

"Has Jasmine gone on strike—I mean, over Nicky?" Charlie asked.

The query made him frown. "More or less. Currently, she's gone up to London, but she doesn't want him back. Pro tem he's a boarder, non-fee-paying and not particularly welcome." The drawer of the supplies cupboard closed with a bang.

Charlie tried to withstand his distant manner. It was almost as though she had offended. With some trepidation she asked what had happened to Hannibal.

"What you saw," Kenneth answered briefly. "And that's more than I did. He was over it when I got there. We took him down the drive, slowly of course, but he coped. Lost his hind legs once, but apart from that no trouble. It was a heart attack, of course. Next time he may not be so lucky." His eyes fell on the package she had left. "What's this? Who left it?"

Charlie took a breath. It should have been a pleasant moment. But it was splintering fast. "I did, actually. I got it at the fête."

"For me?" Kenneth was staring at her. Not a particle of gratification showed in his face. "You mean you bought this whatever-it-is for me? I wish you hadn't."

Sometimes the deeper the hurt the calmer the response. Charlie heard a voice that she hardly recognised as her own. It said composedly : "Yes, I can see that. But don't worry, it's only a tiny thing and it won't bite."

It was humiliating in the extreme. He was embarrassed, he thought she was getting above herself. It had seemed a friendly gesture and it was all wrong, all hatefully wrong.

Kenneth had not touched the little parcel. He was still looking at her.

"That's not what I meant," he said evenly. "It was kind of you, but in the circumstances somewhat embarrassing. I think we should forget about it till you hear what I've got to say. Sit down," he added perfunctorily.

She did so, her cheeks burning with mortification.

"We've traversed this ground before," Kenneth said not unkindly. "It concerns age and suitability. I know there are nine years between us on the calendar; experience is beginning to show that they might as well be light years. I have to ask myself can I afford that difference."

Hurt turned to bewilderment. "Please don't talk in riddles. I haven't the least idea what you're talking about."

"All right, I'll be blunt." He looked at her straightly. "You're kind-hearted and willing and you have a way with you. I thought this practice could very well do with that. In short, I know my own lack. But when it comes to blabbing my actions, at least my ill-judged ones, all over the village, then I have to ask myself what more damage will be done if I let you stay."

It was still a mystery, but five words of it hit her like a whiplash.

"If you let me stay? What makes you think I want to after this?"

"Steady, steady!"

"I won't steady! You're not talking to a horse." It was happening again, that bubbling loss of control so foreign to the logical competent nurse in the London clinic.

"I know that, more's the pity. Horses can be bridled. Your tongue evidently can't."

"I still don't know what you're talking about," Charlie snapped. "What is my tongue supposed to have done?"

"Talked about that damned fox. I was called to the Cheese last night. Their bitch was whelping and had got into difficulties. When I'd finished with her I went into the bar for a drink. It was something of a shock to be quizzed about my new 'vermin ward'." He mistook her stupefaction for guilt and went heavily on. "I've only myself to blame, I know that, but I thought you'd have the sense to realise that when one is fallible one doesn't want it broadcast."

"Who says I did?" Charlie put in.

"Bill Peake."

She had never heard of the man. "He named me?"

"Not in so many words. He called you my 'young lady'."

She had chuckled before she could help herself. It was so unexpected and so ludicrous.

"Figure of speech," Kenneth said grimly. "With which I'm not concerned."

Charlie was thinking fast. As she was not the culprit it could only be Samantha. Incredible that Kenneth's thoughts had not gone straight to her—but fortuitous. Samantha was more vulnerable. She reminded Charlie of a bird. A bird chirruped when the sun shone and went to bits at the stroke of a claw. It would be unthinkable to save oneself at the expense of Samantha.

Surprisingly Kenneth sighed. "I don't enjoy this, Charles, but you *were* irresponsible and indiscreet. The fox I'll live down, what concerns me is your making a habit of it.

It's one thing to have a tongue that charms and I appreciate how pleased Guy was with its performance yesterday, but before it runs away with you again perhaps you'd remember the position you came here to fill."

The insinuation that she might gossip in order to ingratiate herself with Jean Wychwood was so absurd that it reduced Charlie to astonished silence. What had made Kenneth remember such a trivial conversation? She hardly knew Guy's mother. Bluntly speaking, she was—in the personal sense—quite unimportant. Whereas Kenneth and the practice ... Oh, *damn!* Tears were pricking her lashes.

"You don't know me at all," she accused bitterly, and took the sweeping brush into reception.

It posed a challenge. How well did she know herself? In London she had never wanted to assert herself, now she seemed to do it all the time. She supposed she had always been sensitive, but had the pain over Don ever hurt like this? At least she had borne it in silence and acted with dignity.

Today she had hardly been able to contain her passion. Another minute and her hand might have won as on Saturday when it had acted on Jasmine with total surprise to them both.

She looked at it stupidly for a second and then went on sweeping.

Nicky was looking for his mistress. Things had happened to him since she had gone away, none of them pleasant. Today's incarceration was the worst. Charlie's heart ached for him.

Once Kenneth was safely off the premises she took the little dog up to the flat. He went at once to her bedroom and wrapped himself in the eiderdown. From the expertise with which he dislodged the pillow and wedged it into his back, it was easy to see that he was no stranger to his mistress's bed. Later when Charlie took him for a walk he demonstrated his lack of upbringing by twisting his leash around her. When they reached home she removed the lead and he flew round the yard like a whirling dervish, barking, and bucking and jumping at the wall.

Mindful of Kenneth's reactions were there to be complaints from the neighbours, she called him to come in.

Naturally he had no intention of giving up so soon, but to show there was no ill feeling he gave her a wave. He did this by sitting up to beg and then extending his forepaws and waving them up and down.

Charlie stood mesmerised. He was out of hand, out of condition and possibly homeless. She was a practical girl and she saw all the eventualities. She also saw Nicky waving at her for dear life, his brown ears flapping and his white tummy bulging like a greedy child's.

"Oh, you clown!" she said huskily. "I mustn't get fond of you—too."

The temptation to let him sleep in the flat was strong. She was glad she had not yielded to it when next morning she heard Kenneth drive into the yard while she was at breakfast. At least he would find the beagle in the downstairs kennels. She had made several firm resolutions about her employer; the chief one was to keep her cool. It was not easy to do this, however, when she opened the door and found a bunch of roses propped against the frame. There was a note with them. "Apologies. But why? Ken."

When she went down to the surgery he was there, checking the contents of his bag. She had wondered what to say and in the end she just said : "Thank you."

"And thank *you*," he returned. "I phoned you last night, as a matter of fact, but you were out. The tile was a delightful surprise. Well, you knew it would be. I've had my spies out for months. And as to the other, I don't understand in the least, but naturally you're exonerated, I'm relieved, I apologise again and the culprit, I promise you will not sit down for a week!"

Charlie had built up a careful edifice. A severe brushing had swept her hair across her small head. She had on a fresh uniform and she was straightening her cuffs. Away went it all. "You don't mean you've beaten Samantha? You couldn't. She's only a child."

"You're not much older," he said uncompromisingly. "And I damn nearly beat you. Oh, very well," he added, making a concession to her shocked face. "I didn't. But she's had a talking to. I don't think she'll forget it in a hurry. I know she's young, Charles, but there's no use shielding her. She must learn to hold her tongue."

At that moment Charlie was having difficulty in holding hers. He was a good father; she still thought of that first Sunday when he and the children had walked down the aisle of the church hand in hand. He was bringing his family up against odds and regardless of personal sacrifice. Jason was very like him, he did things with the same concentration, but Samantha, good as she was at mothering, was much more of a butterfly. She dreamed dreams and she gave her heart. Charlie was sure Samantha took after her mother.

At the fête people had remarked how sad it was that Jason had never had a mother's love, but surely it was Samantha who had suffered most. To lose one's mother when one was five or six must seem like the end of the world.

A lot was being asked of Samantha—was enough being given her in return?

On Tuesdays there was no afternoon surgery. Kenneth employed his time at Corners, an animal welfare home near Cirencester. It had affiliations with the hospital where Charlie had worked and she had met the manager and his wife. Like most of their kind, they were dedicated to their charges and worked like Trojans, sitting up with sick animals, finding homes for strays and generally restoring and comforting.

When Kenneth suggested that this afternoon she should accompany him to Corners it was a delightful prospect. "I'd love to. I know Mr. and Mrs. Brown. They used to come up to the hospital."

"I must see what room they have," he said thoughtfully. "It would be somewhere to put that dog."

"You might be lucky," Charlie told Nick, communicating the suggestion with his dinner. "You'd be able to run about in the fields and you'd have lots of company. I'll keep my fingers crossed for you—that's a promise."

In the meantime the best she could do was to close up the yard and give him ten minutes' freedom. He dashed about barking zestfully and when she looked down at him from the balcony he saw her immediately and took up his 'waving' position. She could imagine what Kenneth would say to such frivolity, but fortunately by the time he returned from lunch the coast was clear. Nicky was back in quarters and she herself ready to step into the car.

Again a surprise was in store. Kenneth switched off and got out.

"My present," he said, smiling. "You don't mind if we delay to hang it? Obviously it must go in the flat."

The space on the wall was waiting. He took hammer and nails from his pocket and threw off his coat.

Charlie looked at the coat. It was the grey herringbone he wore on his rounds and it bore as she had known it would the name of a custom tailor. Kenneth's tastes were classical. He liked pin-checks with narrow dark ties, and plain trousers, charcoal or lovat blue. Today's shirt was a green pin-check, his neck against it was almost chestnut brown.

The nail went cleanly home and the worker stood back to admire.

"They say every picture tells a story," he remarked, "if you get my drift."

She didn't. She knew only that his pleasure was patent and she had been basking in it.

"The unicorn is a fierce beast," Kenneth continued, "with a high goal, and not a bad average. He told the Welsh dragon to push off and he drew his fight with the lion, who to this day has not been able to get rid of him. If I bamboozle you, Charles, do say."

"Not in the least. You're talking about the royal arms," she said demurely.

"And the quiddity of unicorns." His voice changed: "That one seems to have gone for another crown."

She looked at the quaint little head lying so trustingly in the girl's lap. "Yes," she said softly.

"I don't think we should suppose that his nature has changed. They're a tenacious breed."

"I wouldn't disagree." The room seemed to have grown suddenly still and warm.

"Or that because his attitude is one of surrender he has not in fact won a victory. From my personal knowledge of unicorns . . ."

"Great?" Charlie asked gently.

"Great," he answered firmly. "This one has discovered

that he's been fighting with shadows. The things that looked so fearsome are not there any more. You see, not all unicorns are good at handling themselves."

The pause suggested that he was waiting for her to speak.

"If you say so," she murmured.

"What about you saying something, Charles?" he asked softly. "I can only identify with the unicorn."

Charlie had a floating sensation. He seemed to be throwing her a line, but it was so frail, its filaments so exquisitely fine that a breath would snap them. She could not believe such a wild fantasy. She could not dare the shame and embarrassment if she had got the wrong idea and were to say the wrong words. It would be dreadful beyond words. She would feel like dying—on the spot.

She said shakily: "I think the girl was probably very startled and . . ."

The doorbell pealed.

Kenneth said: "Damn. We're closed." But the moment was gone. He added: "I'm sure you're right—she's too young. Now let's see who wants us."

A few strides took him on to the balcony. Charlie never really knew who had interrupted them. She saw her employer lean over the rail and heard his voice making an appointment for the next morning. Whoever it was had come at the right time. Another second and she would have finished the sentence: 'And very, very glad.' *And how wrong she would have been.* Look how carelessly the subject had been dismissed.

The drive to Corners was pleasant if undramatic. There were smoky tops to the hills and the fields were dotted with hay bales.

"After all that," Kenneth said lightly at one point, "I haven't said a proper thank you."

"Oh, I think you did," Charlie parried as lightly. "The roses were beautiful."

"Yes, they are good this year. Let's hope we don't lose Hannibal yet awhile." He grinned.

There was obviously no cause for alarm. He had noticed nothing strange in her manner. She thanked heaven that she had been able to keep it as casual as his own.

117

Corners with its rest fields for pensioner horses and ponies was a heartwarming place. Mrs. Brown remembered her and seemed pleased to see her again and it was wonderful to see so many contented animals and hear so many stories with happy endings.

Kenneth handed out pills and lotions from his bag and there were some minor operations. He extracted three decaying teeth from a black cat, cleaned out two pairs of ears and gave a couple of injections.

"You know he does all this for free," Mrs. Brown confided. "He's entitled to take his fee, of course, but I've heard he never does."

They were on the point of leaving when Kenneth went back for a further word with Mr. Brown. Charlie, loth to get out of the sunshine and into the car one minute before it was necessary, stood listening as Mrs. Brown told yet another tear-jerking tale. She glanced up as a third car joined the two already parked. Out of it stepped a figure in jeans, sneakers and a denim bomber jacket.

Charlie looked casually, froze and looked again. Don, she recalled, had always liked to dress for the part on field work.

He had seen her now and was coming over. It was not really such a coincidence. Corners had many an intake of patched-up deserving cases from the London hospital and plainly some such matter was on the agenda today.

"Charlotte, what a piece of luck!" The well-remembered voice sounded. Don seized her by the shoulders and kissed her warmly. "You look beautiful. Why aren't you pining for us? It's not fair!"

"Who says I'm not pining?" Charlie retorted with spirit.

"Your face says it," he accused. "Girlie, if that's pining it's the best beauty treatment I've seen. No, seriously, Charlotte, this is great. What brings you to Corners? I'm here for Tom Lemon."

Charlie was explaining when she saw Kenneth back at the car. "There's my boss now. Terribly sorry, Don, I must dash."

It had been a whirlwind meeting. She was still flushed with the excitement of it as she ran over to join Kenneth. "Sorry to keep you. That was a friend from London, from the hospital."

Don had followed. He berated her yet again for running away. There was nothing for it but to introduce them. "Ken, this is Don Harris. Don, Kenneth Carr, my boss."

"Hail and farewell, I'm afraid," Kenneth said, shaking hands. "We have another call to make before five." He looked from Don to Charlie somewhat curiously. She wondered if the name had registered. He was not stupid and Jasmine had referred to Don that evening in the church at Sedge. It was quite probable Ken had remembered and perhaps in today's circumstances no bad thing that he should. Then at least if he should ever think back to her awkward reaction over the unicorn there was no fear he would link it with himself.

"Look, don't just take off," Don complained amusingly. "Give me your phone number. I'll ring you at the weekend."

"Is that a special friend of yours?" Kenneth asked as they headed along the Fosse Way. As Charlie had expected, Don's name had not gone unmarked. "I think Jasmine mentioned him," he added.

Charlie kept her composure. "I believe she did. Mother had been talking, hadn't she?" Instinct told her that for some reason he had not liked the little he had seen of Don. His clothes, perhaps? They were so opposite to tweed and pin-check. As to the question, it was genuinely hard to answer.

One supposedly broken heart had taken only ten days to mend. But a *friend*, yes, and the little encounter had done a lot for morale.

"It depends what you mean by special," she said carefully. "But yes, I suppose so. We used to go out together. He's very bright, you know, even if he doesn't always look professional." She knew she would always feel close to Don on account of that first late duty when the apparently lifeless dog had been brought in.

"His looks are his own affair," Kenneth stated magnanimously. "Unfortunately he has put a spoke in my wheel." He spoke abstractedly, giving his attention to the intersection they were approaching. "Innocently, of course. I gather your ex-bosses are closing their Surrey kennels for renovation and transferring as many boarders as Dick Brown can take. Harris is here to wrap it up. In the circumstances I couldn't persuade them that one rogue beagle is exactly a bonanza. Hence, Charles, we're on our way to hospital to break the news to Mrs. Green."

"What news?" Charlie asked suspiciously.

"That until she's able to take him back, if ever, he rooms, as your mother says, with us."

It was yet another proof that Kenneth Carr's bark was worse than his bite. "I daresay I worry unnecessarily about Samantha," Charlie decided. "She doesn't look in the least an unhappy child."

The schedule was tight, but they beat it, risking a momentary halt in a No Parking area while Charlie dashed into a fruit shop for a bunch of grapes and making the hospital ten minutes before the end of visiting time. Mrs. Green, making progress but still far from robust, was touching in her gratitude. She loved Nicky, but it was clear he was a problem. He had got so big, she said worriedly, and jumped about so much. When he had been given to her he had been such a tiny little fellow. And now someone from the Welfare had suggested she apply for one of the old people's flats where dogs were not allowed. "She said she thought they might let me have a cat." the old lady concluded, brightening. "And I must say a quiet little cat would be more suitable."

"Do you know what I think?" Charlie asked mischievously as they drove on towards Hopehampton. "You've got yourself a beagle."

"I was about to say the same thing to you," Kenneth returned. "How do you feel about sharing a parentage?"

Charlie had allowed herself to entwine with Hopehampton. This evening she was silent from sheer pleasure at the long shadows reaching across the green of the Common and the tranquillity of the grazing ponies. In contrast to yesterday it had been such a good day. She looked happily at Tom Long's Post and the road into the town past the primary school and now the church and the grounds where she had hunted the fox.

And then she sat up, sentiment forgotten. Surely there was something familiar about the small figure slinking through the lych gate, although the school uniform she was wearing changed her normal image considerably.

"Is that Samantha?"

"Where?" Kenneth did not finish. He too had seen his daughter. "What's she been up to now?" He pulled the car into the kerb.

Samantha had not seen them. Her head was down and she was dragging her feet. As the horn sounded sharply she jumped. The customary smile was missing and if ever a little face said : 'Oh no, not him too !' hers did.

Kenneth put a hand behind Charlie, stretched and clicked the door open.

"Why aren't you home?" he demanded as Samantha slid inside. "It's nearly six. Where have you been?"

"I had an appointment." The straw boater with its striped school band did not suit the long pulled-back hair and it was askew which didn't help. The reply hadn't helped either. Charlie thought Kenneth would explode.

"Sam, you've *got* to understand. Mrs. Lane, the home help, goes home at half past five. If I'm a few minutes late getting home I have to know that *you're* there. Who looks after Jason if you're not? Now answer me, what's been happening today? You should have been on the bus at four o'clock. Why weren't you? And what are you doing here?"

It was as Charlie had suspected. All the stress was on Jason. Samantha's woebegone appearance passed unnoticed. As the cross-examination proceeded she could have shaken Kenneth. Granted, Mrs. Lane had been inconvenienced, it was unjust to assume that she would ever walk out and leave Jason unattended, yet over and over again this point was hammered home.

At last she could stand it no longer. "Ken, I'm sure Sam knows that. What was the appointment, Sam? Explain to Daddy."

"It was . . ." Samantha swallowed. "It was with Mr. Clark. To sing for him. To get into the choir." Mr. Clark was organist at the parish church.

Oh no ! Charlie thought pitifully. Samantha's voice was so untuneful. What must it have sounded like? But it was the thing she wanted above all. Here indeed could be small tragedy.

On Kenneth's part there was a startled pause and then uproarious laughter.

"You in the choir!" he hooted. "Good grief, Sam, you'll be the death of me!"

Samantha's eyes were her one claim to beauty. They stared back quenched and dull.

"She didn't have to learn it this way," Charlie thought mutinously.

"I *can* sing, Jasmine said I could," Samantha muttered. It was her last line of defence.

"Jasmine is too kind-hearted," Kenneth returned. At least he had stopped laughing. "She didn't want to hurt your feelings. Oh, come on, Sam. There's no harm done except to Mr. Clark's blood pressure. We'll still find a use for you." He gave his daughter a smile the warmth of which could not be denied and drove on.

"He's very fond of her, he's going home now to cook them a good supper," Charlie reflected stalwartly as she was dropped in the surgery yard. For all that, concern for Samantha could not be wholly quietened.

CHAPTER NINE

A FEW days passed. No emergencies came to the surgery and since Don's promised telephone call had not materialised Nicky had all of Charlie's social life. He enjoyed every moment.

Since Tuesday he had come up in the world, literally as well as figuratively. The balcony of the flat was a good place from which to bark at sparrows and incoming patients. Every morning he took Charlie for a short walk, every evening he took her for a long one. Between times he watched for her.

"He's really doing well," Charlie reported to Kenneth on Friday. "He knows Heel now and he walks beautifully on the lead."

"Charles, I watched you coming down Well Hill last night," Kenneth returned sorrowfully. "And I'm afraid that swan is a goose. He nearly had you off your feet."

"That must have been the time he saw the lion," Charlie improvised wildly. "There was one, you know—running after us. I didn't see it, but Nicky did. He was saving my life."

"Was he indeed?" Kenneth's look softened. "I think I'd choose a better protector." He snapped the lock of his case and moved away. At the door he turned. "You're sure it wasn't a unicorn?"

She had just closed up for lunch break when the phone rang. It was Don. His parents lived in Somerset and he was going home for the weekend. Tomorrow he would come over to Hopehampton. "Consider yourself fully booked," he advised gaily.

The old words came automatically to Charlie's tongue. "Fine. I'll look forward to it." Behind them was a strange niggle of disappointment.

Did she want to be committed? She had planned to take Nicky out. Don meant what he said, they would drive off somewhere and probably have a late night. "I hope he

123

doesn't want me on Sunday too," she thought, and stopped. The wish had come almost unthinkingly. It was shattering in its implications.

For weeks love and Don had been synonymous, but only now in the past few days she was beginning to know the game. Love had to be the rough with the smooth, the bad times with the good, the fireside only after the day's toil. It was the elixir that transformed a wet winter into moonlight and roses. In short, it was a man who called her 'Charles'.

She gave it to herself cold. "You were hoping he might suggest you both took Nicky for a walk tomorrow. You were wondering if you could ask him and the children to tea on Sunday. You—the girl who wanted to live in a backwater and watch the world go by! Well, look at yourself, crazy horse, you're in love up to your tonsils!"

There was only one prescription. Put it down. It was providential that Don was coming next day. He was no more serious about her now than he had been a few weeks ago, so there was no risk of hurting him, but it was imperative that she cure herself, imperative too that she should not be too much alone. Kenneth's compassion was easily roused, she wanted no more solicitous enquiries.

When he came back from lunch he had Jasmine with him. She had begged a lift into town to pick up her car which was being serviced. It would not be ready for another half hour, so she had come to wait in Reception.

"Have a pear, mouse," she invited, opening her shopping bag and placing a large ripe beauty on the desk. "Ken tells me he's sold you the pup. Aren't you a brave little soul?"

"I don't think so," Charlie said boldly. "Nicky is settling very well."

"Ah, where have I heard those words before?" Jasmine sighed.

"Charles has quite a way with him. I don't think we need worry," Kenneth put in unexpectedly. "By the way, Charles, before I forget, keep tomorrow free." He was taking Max to compete in obedience tests at a nearby Dog Show and had thought they might make it a family outing.

"What he means is," Jasmine explained, "he needs someone to mind the children while he's in the ring."

"Not entirely," Kenneth corrected smoothly. "There are other considerations. Well, Charles, can you make yourself available?"

Despite all her sensible resolutions she could have wept. "I'm so sorry, I'm not free. Don has just phoned."

The pause was infinitesimal. "Don't worry, no harm done. I just thought you'd be interested—as an object lesson."

"I'd have loved it and it would have been useful." She knew he was thinking of Nicky.

"In that case why not get Don to take you! He should find it interesting too. I'll give you a handbill." She could see that already he was dismissing the subject.

Just one of those things, Charlie told herself. She simply must not mind so much, especially if she wanted to stay in her job.

Meantime Jasmine was leaning forward, her dark hair dropping over her tanned cheek. "Perhaps I might audition for the part. You'll need someone to keep an eye on the children."

"Of course," Kenneth said readily. "Glad to have you, you know that."

It was stating the obvious. Charlie knew what pleasure it must give him to find Jasmine making even a small overture to country life.

It was not at all certain that Don would comply. As a vet he was an individual, brilliant in the theatre, not so interested in the unspectacular ailments like hair ball, loose teeth or gastritis.

Kenneth by contrast was an animal lover. All that mattered when he had a little patient in his hands was to find the cause of its discomfort and make it well.

As it happened, however, Don was more amenable than she had expected and agreed to the Dog Show provided they found somewhere swinging for the evening.

His smile was polite as he held the door for her. She felt vaguely that he was disappointed in her appearance. The image didn't change much, she owned guiltily, bright short hair, long legs, brief linen look skirt in emerald green, flowery blouse in white and emerald. The skirt and blouse were new, purchased in a boutique with red sunblinds near the Market House, and she had purposely avoided the blue shades she wore so often. The strong gay green was different and she had been pleased with it, but somehow she knew Don would have liked her to look more sophisticated.

Nicky was another difficulty. "I would like to bring him Don if you don't mind too much," she submitted. "He's been shut up all the morning and he won't get his walk tonight. He'll be no trouble, I promise."

She could see it was a struggle, but Don was good-hearted. "Well, seeing where we're going I suppose they can hardly refuse him admission!"

It was the signal for Nicky to tear into the middle of the yard, sit up on his hind legs and wave with his front paws.

"Did you ever see a dog do that before?" Charlie asked rashly.

"I'd prefer not to!" Don retorted. "He's obscene. Look at his paunch!"

A drive of about twelve miles brought them to the show grounds. Nicky had been restless in the car, trying to scramble from back to front and breathing warmly on their necks. He was ready for anything when he saw it was time to get out. Charlie had intended leaving him in the car and slipping out at intervals to give him an airing, but the car park was a good stretch from the show ring and was in blazing sun. Even with a slit of the window open he would roast.

"In for a penny, in for a pound," Don said resignedly as Nicky pranced through the turnstile.

It was a big show and in three rings judging was already in progress. With such a large crowd it was not surprising that at first sight there seemed to be no sign of Kenneth and his party, but, after some minutes, as they stood watching a class of Toys, Charlie felt a sharp tug on the leash in her hand. Nicky had caught a glimpse of Max and had darted forward to greet him.

The German Shepherd as usual walked attentively and close to his master. Surely it was a good sign that Nicky with such a lot to learn was virtually mad about Max. In

126

Woodsgift he had always made a beeline for the Carr garden and if the barricades which Kenneth used to secure Jason were in position he would stand at them for hours barking and wagging frantically at his hero.

Today noses were duly rubbed and tails were sniffed. It was Charlie's belief that Max returned the little beagle's feelings. Max's owner, however, did not look so pleased.

"I didn't expect you to bring the dog," he said shortly. "Bit of a risk, I'd have thought."

"Charlie the lionhearted," Don quipped.

The last time they'd shared a joke about a lion Kenneth had followed it with that funny little crack about the unicorn. He was making no jokes this afternoon. "I hope you know what you're doing. Stacks could be blown, I warn you, if anything happens."

"The car is right in the sun," Charlie said defensively. "I had to bring him."

"Well, be careful, that's all," Kenneth warned again. Suddenly he smiled. "Blindfold him if you see that lion coming!"

He and Max had been the vanguard. Jasmine had now caught up. Don was frankly goggling and as Charlie made the necessary introductions she remembered how the first time she had met Jasmine she had thought these two would make a good pair. There was no doubt of it now that she saw them together. Two 'candles' drawing the eyes of every moth in the crowd.

Don's side-vented corduroy jacket was a vivid marmalade gold. Jasmine's full-length dress was diamond-patterned with as many colours as Harlequin. Its low neck displayed her tropical suntan, its tight-fitting top emphasised her breasts. It was a departure from the shirts and neck chains she usually wore, and yet entirely in keeping. Jasmine was always theatrical.

To Charlie's surprise she herself on this occasion was not addressed as 'mouse'. "Nice to meet you, Don," Jasmine was saying cordially. "Charlie told me about you. I hoped you'd get down soon. I'm afraid it's been a lonely stretch for her. Come on, Ken," she added. "We mustn't play goosberry."

"Not 'we'—you," Kenneth corrected. "It's time Max and

I checked in."

He started to move off. Another 'candle', Charlie thought admiringly. Nothing could have been more becoming to his tanned features than the lightweight parchment jacket and sand-coloured polo-necked sweater. He had a flair for dress, though he never went outside the classic syndrome.

"Best of luck," she called, and he halted to say: "Thank you," and to wave.

"Please don't go," Don was saying to Jasmine. "If you do I shall think you don't like the look of me."

In minutes it seemed to Charlie that she herself had ceased to exist. Don had made the first nibble, Jasmine returned it by training on him her complete battery of charm. When Charlie enquired for Samantha and Jason she had to raise her voice and repeat the question before she was even heard. Then Jasmine answered carelessly: "You'd never guess, would you? We bumped into Steph! Do you know, I'm beginning to suspect do-gooders don't trust me."

Charlie was indignant. "Stephanie isn't a 'do-gooder', that's not fair. She just tries to help."

"So she does love, so she does. And I am enormously grateful. At the precise moment we met her Jason was roaring for icecream and Samantha's beady little eyes were going in the same direction. I assure you I was ready to be relieved. Not my thing at all, I'm afraid."

"Nor mine!" Don said heartily.

Charlie was silent. She had little doubt that this was the real Jasmine speaking, but it contrasted forcibly with her previous treatment of the children. And the careless manner in which she had encouraged poor Samantha to think she could sing was part and parcel of it. Hypocrisy was bad enough; last Tuesday had bordered on tragedy.

By this time the dogs and their handlers were beginning to assemble in the ring. Collies and German Shepherds predominated with a sprinkling of Labradors, a golden retriever and a tiny Yorkshire terrier who received a special cheer from the onlookers.

Charlie watched the first pair entranced. The dog, Jim, was a Border collie and to her untutored eyes his performance was impressive. A couple of men behind her, however, commented more critically. Jim had had one crooked sit and he dropped his article after picking it up. That, she learned, would cost him two marks. He was followed by a German Shepherd bitch on whose walking the commentators waxed positively euphoric. Certainly the attentive way in which she looked up at her mistress all the time was very appealing. The Yorkshire was an obvious favourite with the crowd. When the test ended he jumped from the sitting position like an uncoiled spring and finished halfway up his handler's arm.

Kenneth and Max were number twelve. Their first test was excellent. Max walked close heel, his tongue lolling; not even the bitch had looked up more attentively. Kenneth strode easily, his suntanned face intent. When he walked away Max waited, presenting a nice straight sit. The pick-up as Kenneth walked past him again was perfect and at the end of the field he turned as neatly as though he were his master's shadow.

"This one makes nothing of it, does he?" the critic behind Charlie remarked. It was encouraging because so far all his prophecies had been correct.

"Isn't Max a super dog?" she appealed to her companions.

"I'm just looking at *your* super dog, mouse," Jasmine said kindly. "Do you know his collar is loose? He could slip it." She stooped down.

"Mind that gorgeous dress," Don chimed in, and stooped in his turn. It was just what he had *not* said to Charlie.

Not that she minded that. Beside the horror of Nicky getting loose, compliments were of no importance at all. "Is it really loose? How could it be?" She had fastened the collar herself and she was always very careful.

"Yes, it really is," Don retorted. "Now what do you say?"

Charlie said nothing. She was still incredulous and his head was in her line of vision.

"All right, Don, I've got it," Jasmine reported. Don stood up and Charlie felt Nicky's body brush warmly against her leg. Next instant there was an exclamation. "Oh *no!*" Jasmine had the collar in her hand. "My God, stop him!" she shouted.

129

It took only a moment. There was the confusion of Jasmine's long skirt which threatened to trip her up. There was Don helping to steady her and the man behind them saying : "Got away, has he? Which way did he go?" Above all there was Nicky, charmed by his unexpected freedom and suddenly showing that he was a miniature foxhound and foxhounds ran for their living.

Charlie was sure Nicky had never run so fast in his life. "Please, someone, catch him!" she called imploringly, and started in pursuit.

Without his collar Nicky was slippery and dodgy. No one could hold him. He got through and there before his eyes was the very chap he'd been looking for—Max. With a bay of triumph Nicky bounded into the ring. A few hands tried to grab him and failed.

The scene spread horrifyingly as Charlie reached the perimeter of the field. It was the test for Distance Control. Away out in the centre of the grass sat Max, straight-backed, feet together, regal and alone. He was to sustain the pose for two minutes with Kenneth out of sight. 'Perfectly stationary' was the requirement. Max might have been turned to bronze.

With all eyes riveted on him, he was waiting for just one voice.

But—oh, dear lord—he was *not* alone. Nicky's white capering shape was making straight for him. With an excited bark he reached him and circled round, 'wow-wow'-ing and flagging his tail.

Max did not move.

As Charlie started forward, her heart thumping, to try and drag Nicky away, several people motioned her back. They thought she might do more harm than good.

It was agonising. She stood, clammy-palmed, while from across the field Kenneth gave the 'Down' command. How could Max hear it, Charlie fretted; Nicky's cheerful volleys were still rending the air.

Max heard. He went down, elbows firm, tail quiet, tongue lolling. He looked like a Landseer lion. Nicky started to dance.

By this time amusement was rippling round the crowd. So far as she could judge with the distance between them it was not shared by Kenneth. His light jacket accentuated his shoulders, his face was set. He was as motionless as his dog.

Luckily at that moment something in the crowd caught Nicky's attention and he bounded off to investigate. Charlie trying to follow him, found herself wedged in. There was nothing to do but wait until the control tests finished.

The final part of these brought all dogs into the ring. The requirement was that on command they should lie flat with all legs extended and sustain this position on their own for ten minutes. All went smoothly. The handlers commanded their dogs and left them. Charlie looked at the circle of prone bodies and allowed herself to breathe again. The strain had been terrible, but now peace reigned supreme. She looked at Max, apparently lifeless in his pose, and with a sigh of thankfulness closed her eyes.

She opened them on a roar of laughter. The circle was unbroken, to their credit no dog had moved, but then not all were in the line of fire. It was at Max's side that Nicky sat, on his hind legs, barking and 'waving' at the company. The more they looked at him the more pleased he was.

Nicky liked a bit of life around him. He was telling them so and he had a captive audience.

When the test finished he executed a kind of polka round Kenneth and Max and as they left the ring he brought up the rear. To Charlie's fearful eyes, Kenneth's face had never looked stonier. She made a futile grab at Nicky which, being collarless, he eluded easily.

"Ken, I—don't know what to say."

"Sorry would do for a start," he commented coldly. "And perhaps some realisation of just what you put at risk."

"I know," she said penitently. "I do, Ken. I know how hard you worked and what it means . . ."

"I'm not talking about myself," he cut in impatiently. "Max is used to him. The others were much more vulnerable. Any one of them could have been put right off his stroke. A show like this isn't just play, you know. It's hard cash to a lot of people—not a circus as you appear to think."

"Of course I don't." Fair dues, she had to take some blame, but this was unjust. "And I *am* sorry. I know it was terrible, but I still don't understand how it happened. Jasmine was tightening his collar, she said it was loose, I..." All at once the moment seemed to be electric.

"I don't know why you had to bring him at all. I warned you," he reminded. "Take him away and hold on to him. Or put him in the car where he ought to have stayed in the first place."

Every word of it she knew was true. If she had pursued the point Don might have found a space for the car in the shade. But she had not asked him. She had just done the one thing her training most vehemently decried, allowed her heart to get the better of her sense.

Back with Don and Jasmine, she found, not unexpectedly, that Don who had come to the show on sufferance was now reluctant to leave before it closed. He tossed her the car keys and said carelessly : "That one—and you have to push it. It sticks."

Knowing Don's form, it was amusing. If he thought, however, that he was making any real impression on Jasmine he could not have been more wrong. Jasmine collected men as some folk collect souvenirs, but you would have to be very dense not to know when her feelings were truly engaged.

She might still be fighting the surrender to country life, but she was Kenneth's girl, jumpy if a stranger came on her patch, a dangerous enemy.

"She has no need to worry," Charlie thought flatly.

Nor had she herself any need to hurry. No one would miss her and she no longer had much desire to watch the rest of the proceedings.

Nicky was quiet after his *coup*. She had brought his dish and a water bottle and she gave him a drink before shutting him up. The sun's rays were no longer hitting the car and she owned once more that she had been at fault. Thirty minutes ago, at the latest, it would have been safe to take him back if she had thought to check. It was just one more proof of the way she had changed.

The last test—Discrimination—was well under way when she got back to the show ring and there seemed little point in searching out Don and Jasmine. She stood alone, still wishing she could hide away. Everyone, she was sure, would recognise her as the girl whose careless handling could have wrecked months of work. It was the last straw when she saw Jean Wychwood further along the ring. As usual Guy's mother was looking elegant. She was wearing the camel shade for which obviously she had a liking; today it was a softly tailored suit. The thought of Jean's cool tongue at that moment was too much to be borne. Charlie returned the smile and then looked away.

The discrimination test followed the usual plan. Each dog in turn sniffed a rag which had been handled by one of the judges and then had the task of selecting the one out of ten other rags which bore the same scent. The watchers knew that the same judge had rubbed rag number ten and that rags six and eight had been rubbed by other judges and laid as decoys. The time allowed was two minutes extended so long as the dog kept working.

The last dog to go before Max was a Border collie. His handler, a girl, rubbed the scented rag on his chest and the dog went briskly to work. He sniffed for a moment at the decoy in place number eight, went past it to number ten, picked up the trophy and padded firmly home. He had no star quality, but he was correct, a straight sit for the give-back, then round the handler from right to left and an upward look. Even when she patted him he did not smile.

The crowd were waiting for Max. Not only was he leading on points but his impeccable behaviour under stress had won all hearts. There was a whisper of anticipation as Kenneth bound the scented rag over his nose. But it was not to be. Incredibly the maestro made a mistake.

He was, as usual, a joy to watch, his movement so fluid that he seemed to pour down the course, and he was quick and confident. Someone beside Charlie gave an 'A-ah' of disappointment. Charlie herself was stunned. Max looked so beautiful and so intelligent as he sat straight as a rush in front of Kenneth and presented him with the decoy from number six. 'Don't tell him,' she prayed passionately. 'Don't let him know.'

Max would guess nothing from the disappointed silence of the crowd. There was one person only who could demolish him. He went round Kenneth's legs like a shadow, appeared again at his left hand and laughed up.

The response was immediate. His head was patted, his ears pulled.

"Good lad," said the voice he loved. "Nice work."

Everyone saw Kenneth's grin as he tossed in his hand the rag which had cost them fifty marks.

CHAPTER TEN

AS she and Don drove back to the town Charlie wondered if it would not be a kindness to release him from the rest of the date. As things stood, she felt so depressed and remorseful that it would be impossible to be good company.

A hint to this effect, however, was firmly overruled. "Grow up, Charlotte, you can't win 'em all. And that's the word of an expert!"

He was right, of course. Staying at home to gloom was no way to live. And no one could doubt that Don made a success of living. She could learn from him.

The mood carried her through the evening. At first it was hard work to produce even a veneer of gaiety, but as the night wore on her answers became more pat and she fancied Don looked at her approvingly.

"You've changed," he remarked as they finished dinner in the distinctly pricey hotel to which he had brought her. "Two weeks ago you were just a kid and you thought I was the greatest. Now you don't even like me and you're suddenly making an impact. Something has given you a tongue. Which," he drawled, "combined with your other not inconsiderable talents interests me quite a bit."

"But you still don't like my dress!" she shot in, laughing. It, too, was new, a multi-coloured border cotton with a tie of the same material. Again she had seen him glance at it when she joined him.

He did not deny the charge. "Haven't you got a long one? You'd look great." It was all extremely good-humoured. "Trust Uncle Don. He knows."

"Yes, I'm quite sure he does," Charlie mocked.

At the same time it made sense. She was twenty-one, not bad-looking and not a bad shape. Did she want to go on for the next ten years giving the impression that she was 'just a kid'? Acquaintanceships, after all, need not be permanent; Don's never were, nonetheless everyone liked him and, most important of all, nobody had to pity him.

No one had to feel responsible or worried that he might be sitting at home with nowhere to go.

And here he was, her ticket to the new life.

"I'll buy it," she said gaily.

"What?" Don parried. "A long dress?"

Why not, she thought recklessly, you had to begin somewhere.

His weekend, it seemed, was a longer break than she had realised. He would not be going back to London until Tuesday. Sunday had to be set aside for his parents. It was their anniversary and his married sister was coming for the day. "Monday," he said thoughtfully. "You get that dress, girlie, and I'll come and inspect."

"Come to supper," Charlie invited. "It will be good for me." Cooking for one made you lazy. It was a thing that she did well, but lately, without the stimulus of her mother to share them, meals for herself had lacked variety.

"Indeed," Don agreed heartily. "It will be, I promise."

Sunday morning was peaceful. Charlie was nursing two cases which had had operations the previous day. They would be going home soon and at this stage needed only replenishment of their hot water bottles plus a bit of petting and some coaxing to take food. She had braced herself to meet Kenneth should he come in to see them, but this did not happen.

She made some preparations for Monday's supper and on impulse phoned her mother for a chat. Ruth Lavender was transparently pleased to hear that Don had kept his promise. She hoped Charlie would soon manage a weekend at home. "Any chance of next Saturday? You could take Don to a show. You know Bill always has tickets." Bill Lowry was a colleague. He ran the magazine's show page.

It was a little more than Charlie had bargained for. The present was not the best time to ask Kenneth for a favour and the care of Nicky for a weekend posed problems. On the other hand it would be nice to see home. Perhaps she could go up by the first train on Sunday.

"Whatever you like, baby. We could meet you at Reading," her mother said accommodatingly. Who 'we' would turn out to be was uncertain, but Charlie was used to that.

She had promised Nicky a long walk to make up for yesterday's long confinement to barracks. There was no use keeping up the hate. He had been no more than a pawn in the game.

Just as they were setting out the phone rang. "Miss Lavender?" a cool voice asked. "This is Jean Wychwood. I was wondering if you would care to come round this afternoon and have a cup of tea with me."

It was so unexpected that Charlie did not answer immediately. Her silence was misconstrued. "Perhaps you have another engagement?"

"No. I was just taking the dog for a walk."

"Splendid. Then you can walk him over here."

"Oh no, I . . ." No jolly fear, Charlie was thinking. "I don't think so. I'll leave him behind."

"My dear child, there's no necessity for that. I like dogs."

Charlie made a last attempt. "It's just that Nicky is a little unpredictable," and was as decisively deposed. "Then we can be forearmed. That's settled, then. I'll expect you both about four."

"Behave or I'll kill you," Charlie threatened Nicky.

Her feelings were mixed as she took off jeans and jacket and replaced them with the new cotton dress. Its colours—black and white, copper and tangerine—were a change for her and the print was clever with a rich black and copper border. She felt sedate as she set out, forcing Nicky to walk quietly on a short leash.

The white dower house looked its usual chaste self. She had expected to see Guy, but when she rang the bell Jean Wychwood herself came to the door.

"I'm so pleased you could come," she said cordially. "As you probably know, Guy is away this weekend, so I'm alone."

In Charlie's mind the one big question was in what place could Nicky do least damage? She had guessed that he would like going to Woodsgift, it was an old haunt and he had not been long about saluting the shiny black shoe-scraper on the doorstep. Now as he frolicked into the hall her heart sank. "Mrs. Wychwood, I can't help worrying about him. Could I tie him up somewhere outside?"

She was not to know how appealing she looked. The round curve to her cheek was schoolgirlish, so were the rather long arms that kept jerking with the tugs on the leash. "She's a pretty child, I can't help liking her," Jean Wychwood thought. "She reminds me somewhat of myself."

"If you're thinking about yesterday," she said briskly, "I should forget it. No harm was done."

Charlie could not dismiss it as easily. To her, the reason for Max's poor performance was there in front of them, lolling his tongue and no doubt at this moment planning a mischief. He should never have got loose, she murmured, it was a terrible misfortune.

"I wonder how it happened," her hostess hazarded shrewdly. "Perhaps he pulled against your fingers."

"Oh no, I ..." Charlie hesitated. "As a matter of fact Jasmine was tightening his collar. He got his neck out."

"Ah." Jean had most intelligent eyes. If she had been looking for an answer she seemed to have found it. "I don't care for Miss Buck," she added. "Any more than I care for the hideous colour she has put on the house. It's limestone, you know, like the cottages. We would never have interfered with the natural stone, it weathers so beautifully. I, of course, am a conservationist, very often misjudged. People these days have little feeling for the past." It might have been Charlie's grandmother speaking.

Indeed as minute succeeded minute, she felt this more and more. The room with its lofty ceiling and tall sash windows was very gracious. In the garden wall the window was like a door. It stretched from floor to ceiling and ran on sash cords. Outside, the narrow garden had Mediterranean brightness, much of it swarming from clay pots and troughs.

Nicky was allowed into the garden while the tea was in progress.

"I wonder if you have been long enough in Hopehampton, Miss Lavender, to make up your mind about it?" Jean Wychwood enquired. "I understand my son-in-law has taken you on a month's trial and vice versa."

Charlie admitted that such was the case. "So there's more to it than the place. But as far as that goes, it was love at first sight."

"Then you wouldn't mind settling here permanently?"

It was a difficult question. Charlie tried to evade it.

"My dear child," she was told brusquely, "you must know what I'm driving at. It doesn't primarily concern Kenneth."

Charlie supposed that riding up to a difficult fence might feel like this. She thought she saw where they were heading, but she was not sure.

"Mrs. Wychwood," she said gently, "if I said I don't know would you understand?"

There was a pause. Jean Wychwood did not move. Her dark eyes peaked at the corners. She was pale but determined. "May I call you Charlie?"

"Please do."

"Then, Charlie," a wintry smile twisted the corners of the mouth, "if I said that I'm giving you my blessing would that make things clearer?"

Jasmine had once said maliciously that Jean was looking for a suitable wife for Guy. Then it had seemed a tasteless joke, now it was touching. Charlie felt intuitive about Jean Wychwood.

"Thank you, Mrs. Wychwood," she said softly. "I must tell you that what you have suggested is unlikely, but I'm very grateful and I hope that ... if I do stay I may come and see you and perhaps ask your advice about things. I should value that very much."

"And so would I, Charlie, though I had hoped—oh well, never mind. That's your own affair. My name is Jean, by the way—to my friends."

Once over the first hurdle and the rest was easy, not excepting a reference to their unfortunate first encounter over Lady Turpin's cat. "Where I must admit I was totally in the wrong," Jean allowed. "As a matter of fact you interested me from that moment. You were not impolite, but you stuck to your guns. I thought you had backbone." She smiled. "And you have. I've been watching you. You're not very big, but you can be fierce. I saw what happened when Jasmine Buck tried to cheat you at the fête. I thought she would pay you back—that's why yesterday didn't surprise me. Oh, that woman!" Teeth clicked exasperatedly. "How I do dislike her. Kenneth must break away from the past, I suppose, dear knows it all but crucified him, but if I thought *she* would ever get my grandchildren . . ."

The voice rasping into silence had spattered words like tracer bullets. Charlie felt herself recoil. 'It all but crucified him', Jean had said. What had she meant? The craving to know was all the more shocking because it was in no sense the business of anyone outside the Wychwood family.

What Jean had gone on to say was equally astonishing. "You're fond of Samantha and Jason?" Charlie asked hesitantly.

"Should I not be?" For a second the former tartness returned. "Oh, I suppose I play the role that woman allots me, the old witch in the wood. That's her pleasant name for me, I've heard her. And the children copy. They're besotted, of course, as she intends they should be. And naturally I won't compete."

Oh, this is a mess, Charlie thought hopelessly. The adults were being so true to type and in the middle were the children, Samantha particularly so much in need of a loving grandmother.

She found herself looking almost resentfully at her companion and the waistcoat suit she had been wearing yesterday at the show. Its soft camel colour toned beautifully with the dark blue and white striped shirt and the long double necklace of gold and dark blue. Jean Wychwood always looked right and so did her hair—brushed softly but crisply about her well poised head.

Clothes, colours, hair—*especially hair*—did it. All at once Charlie fizzled into indignant fire.

"My father died when I was a baby and Mummy had to go back to work, but we had Gran. I know now what a nuisance I must have been. All *she* ever let me know was that she loved me. I don't mean she was sentimental. I was always getting told off for looking untidy or losing my hair slide. You see, she cared how I looked and she knew me. She lent me wonderful books and she talked to me. I used to tell her everything. I don't know what Samantha tells you, but *I* know that she wants a maxi dress and that she'd give the world if she could sing in tune and look at

140

her hair—personally it makes me weep. Oh, I'm sorry . . ."
She had said too much. She would never be asked again.

And something worse was happening at this moment,
something that momentarily at least put Jean Wychwood's
reaction to the outburst into the background.

Out in the garden Nicky had discovered the hose and
was attempting to chew it.

Charlie leaped through the window. There were teeth
marks, but she did not think they had penetrated. Nicky
scampered down the grass, sat up on his hind legs and
waved.

"Not at me you needn't," Charlie said angrily. "I don't
like you."

"Charlie!" The whisper came from just above her head.
"Don't say anything," it went on urgently. "He's waving at
me." Samantha's face, framed by bushes, was looking down
at her. The child was at the boundary hedge which cut
off Kenneth's garden from that of his mother-in-law. "Ssh,"
she cautioned again. "Don't tell her. Don't let her see."

By now Jean's tall figure was hurrying down the path.
Charlie took a chance. "Don't run away, Sam. I'm sure
Gran would like to see you."

Promptly and so easily that she could hardly credit her
ears came her hostess's voice : "Yes, indeed I would, Sam.
Why don't you come in and have tea with us?"

Samantha had been trusting to the bushes to screen her.
Something told Charlie that it was a favourite hidey-hole.
Now she started back : "Thank you very much, but Daddy
says we're not to disturb you."

"But if I invite you?" Samantha was not old enough to
appreciate the spasm that had crossed her grandmother's
face.

"I couldn't come now," she said with thinly disguised
relief. "I'm minding Jason."

Charlie supposed that would end matters. Miraculously
it didn't. Jean's dark eyes looked straight at her granddaughter's green ones. "I know you're a very busy person,
Samantha, but I am sometimes very lonely and I *would*
like your company. I'm sure Miss Lavender would take
charge of Jason for half an hour."

Charlie had brought it on herself. She could not say

that the last place in which she wanted to be found was Kenneth's garden. Happily Jean had an alternative.

"Would you like to give my birds their supper?" she asked as Jason was sighted trotting along imperturbably in his sister's grasp.

"I'm afraid I didn't have time to wash him," Samantha apologised earnestly. She looked longingly at the path that curved down to the water. "He's never been down there. Daddy says it's trespassing."

"Not any more," her grandmother said jerkily. "You may take him wherever you like." She laid her arm on Samantha's shoulders and ushered her into the house.

If I've started something, let it be good, Charlie prayed as she and Jason went carefully down the slope.

Jean had given her grain to scatter and had indicated the doves' customary eating spot. Summoning them was unnecessary. They had been keeping an eye to the arrangements and they swooped, some from the chimneys of the house, some from the dovecote and some, spectacularly, from the trees across the lake. The air whirred with wings. It would have been understandable if Jason had been scared, but once again he was his father's son.

His hands were almost too small to hold the grain, but he threw with gusto, wiping his palm fastidiously on the seat of his pants. To his greedy customers he said severely: "Wash your hands!" and when Charlie wanted to help him up the steps he was instantly offended. "No!" he cried warningly, wrinkling his brow.

It would not be long before this one untied the apron strings, Charlie decided amusedly, as they climbed.

When they got back to the drive, however, amusement died. Samantha as anticipated was still inside the dower house, but another figure was waiting. Leaning on the wall that rimmed the dell, he had, she realised, been watching their ascent. It made her heart sink to see he was unsmiling. Even when Jason broke away and ran to him there was no let-up. Kenneth ruffled his son's head, absently it seemed. His eyes still stayed on Charlie.

"I'd rather you didn't bring him down there," he said curtly. "It's out of bounds."

"Not any more," Charlie returned easily. "Jean has

lifted the ban."

"I didn't know she had one," Kenneth remarked. "I do know that for obvious reasons Samantha is not permitted to take Jason down to the water. That's *my* ruling and it's not up to you, Jean, or anyone else to amend it."

As always the point was unanswerable but need he have couched it so overbearingly? "I'm sorry, I didn't think."

"No harm done." Kenneth was looking at her face. "But I know this monkey." He poked Jason in the ribs. "Where's Sam?"

Charlie had little confidence left. She told her news as though it deserved a rebuff.

Kenneth listened, crinkled his eyes. As always his summing up was enigmatic. "You have a pretty good dipstick, Charles, I'll say that for you, even if you do keep it hidden."

It was an odd moment—incomprehensible, heady. She saw Jason twirl about trying to disengage his hand, but Kenneth stood like a rock, his eyes fixed on her face. They seemed to be imprinting her bright cheeks and the swagger of hair. She had put on a gentle dress, but somehow she still looked a tomboy.

Now to his astonishment his free hand touched the top of her head. "Not a trace," he said whimsically. "It's amazing. I don't know how you unicorns manage nowadays."

"You did say—unicorns?" she stammered.

"Oh yes. What other animal tests a cup for poison?" His hand had dropped to her shoulder. "Charles, I don't know what it is about you. You're the craziest changeling any grandmother ever had, and yet now and then there *are* occasions—and this is one of them—when I'm glad you're not a tile hanging on the wall in my flat."

It was a generous speech. It gave her the credit for preparing Samantha's way into her grandmother's house. As usual it was charmingly phrased. She was rather pleased at being likened to the unicorn who in the legend which the tile portrayed had dipped its horn into the chalice to check for poison.

"Just thought I'd mention it," Kenneth said softly. His head had come closer.

She hardly felt her own movement, it was all so quiet and natural and such a short distance. "It was just a thank-you kiss," she thought as his lips drew away. And—a sad one. It was as though he had kissed her in spite of himself, not because he had wanted or had enjoyed it.

Pain lashed her into speech. "Haven't you got the genders mixed? I thought unicorns were male."

"Thoughts change," he said cryptically. "I put more trust in my second ones."

It was the nearest he had come to admitting that for a few minutes last Tuesday he had had a whimsy about himself and someone other than Jasmine and very different from her. But second thoughts *were* best. Charlie knew how misguided anything else would have been, so it was illogical to mind hearing it put into words. And yet she did mind. The hurt of it was almost intolerable. It took all her control to continue with the speech she had rehearsed.

"I saw the end of the trials yesterday. You must have been very disappointed. Poor Max! I'm afraid Nicky upset him."

"It doesn't follow," Ken said temperately. "Max needs more experience. We'll have another crack next month."

"You still blame me, don't you, for letting Nicky go?"

"Blame is a strong word." His tone was benevolent. "No doubt you were the instrument, but there were extenuating circumstances. Jasmine spoke up for you last night."

"In what way?" Charlie asked warily.

"When I was your age," he said indulgently, "I wouldn't have needed it spelled out. As I see it—and forgive me for my shortsightedness yesterday—you and Don were together on a date. I shouldn't have left Jasmine to play gooseberry and in fact she shouldn't have stayed—we both realise that now. So apologies all round, the matter is closed. Agreed?"

Charlie knew that she should not be surprised by any manifestation of Jasmine's skill, but even with previous experience she had to marvel at the smoothness of tactic. At one stroke it cancelled the real guilt issue, linked her to Don and made Kenneth co-partner with Jasmine. "You mean," she hazarded slowly, "I'm with Don, I don't want anyone else, Jasmine joins us, so I get mad and let Nicky loose."

"I think that's over-simplification," he returned drily. "But to me it seems quite reasonable that your day had been spoiled and consequently you were distrait and off balance. Now I really don't want to hear any more about it. I've told Jasmine so." He glanced at her. "That makes you smile?"

"It makes me laugh," Charlie said coldly. She too could box clever. "You must think I'm very romantic. But as you say, thoughts change and times do too. I don't think you need worry about me—or Don."

There! Kenneth himself had never been more enigmatic. She had said nothing that wasn't true, but she'd given just the picture she'd striven for, the picture of someone heartwhole and able to look after herself. Look at it long enough, she thought hopefully, and she might believe it. Obviously Kenneth already did.

"Good," he said briefly. "Now where's this child of mine?"

CHAPTER ELEVEN

NEXT morning during a lull in surgery Kenneth remarked that he had had a conversation with Jean. She had been looking out for his car and had stopped him as he passed her house. It was to do with Hannibal, the old horse. She had wanted a further examination and a prognosis. "And she was right, which didn't surprise me," Kenneth allowed. The horse's condition had deteriorated perceptibly in the past eight days. It was certain he would get another attack and a worse one quite soon, and this aroused considerations practical as well as humane. "All in all I advised her to have him put down."

"Oh, I am sorry. How did she take it?" Charlie asked pitifully.

"She agreed, of course. She knew it already. There's not much Jean Wychwood doesn't know about horses. The trouble comes when she tries to take command. She wanted it done before Guy got home today, but I had to tell her that wasn't on."

Charlie could see the problem. What she could not fully appreciate was the look on Kenneth's face.

"She seems very fond of you," he said diffidently. "In fact she makes no secret of the fact that she would like you as a daughter-in-law. My advice, for what it's worth, is to take your time."

"I really have no idea . . ." Charlie began.

"What I'm talking about. That I realise," he cut in. "As *you* must accept that I have a duty to—the past. But don't underestimate Jean's gift for seizing the moment." He paused.

The air seemed to tingle. "I must say I like her—very much," Charlie said spiritedly. "And Guy is a dear."

"And will remain so as long as he stays in Hopehampton. It's a domiciliary hazard," Kenneth observed. "Of course, should he ever leave the country as he sometimes threatens to, he just might change into a man." He checked. "But I

146

forgot. You're not romantic, so you'll have figured this out for yourself."

"I think you're laughing at me," Charlie protested. "I did tell you I wasn't born yesterday."

"You weren't by any chance born tonight? Midsummer Eve is so eminently suitable for the birthday of a unicorn."

Charlie had forgotten for the moment that today was Midsummer Eve when the Long Stone out near the Devil's Churchyard was supposed to walk. "What a pity Don is coming to supper! Otherwise I might have gone over to see it."

The twinkle fled from Kenneth's eyes. "Don't try that after dark—or indeed any time if you're by yourself. There's been talk of a Peeping Tom in that area, one or two courting couples are supposed to have been pried on. I didn't take it seriously until last Friday afternoon. I saw two youngsters in the field as I was driving past and a chap standing behind a tree. It could have been nothing, but I didn't care for the way he was looking at them, they were girls about Sam's age, so I stopped and went to investigate. The moment I spoke to him he cleared off without answering. The kids hadn't seen him at all and I didn't want to alarm them but felt I shouldn't take chances, so I marched them back to the road and saw them home. Their mother was in, so I told her about it and then called in at the police station and told them. They took a note of it for the patrol car, but of course it's all rather nebulous. The fact remains, I don't want you to go anywhere that's off the beaten track. I know you take that dog out every night, so please be careful."

"What did the man look like?"

"Very ordinary. He was about thirty, I'd say. Dark. Medium height. His hair was long and he was wearing a green anorak. The point is you can't be sure, so you take no chances. Is that understood?"

It was strange how nearness to a person opened them up. A few weeks ago Kenneth had been 'Mr. Masculinity', her tough infallible employer. Now he was someone who could look bothered. He never opted out of his responsibilities, but sometimes they preyed on him. The flick of an eyelid was enough to tell her this.

"Well, is it? Have I your word?" She jumped at the impatient tone.

"Yes, of course. I'm sorry, I was woolgathering."

"That's just what I'm afraid of," he said uncompromisingly. "That dog would be no use, remember. However, time's getting on. You'd better send in the next patient."

A great deal had to be accomplished in the lunch break. Charlie tried not to see Nicky's anticipatory scurries to the door. Today there would be no time for his customary walk round the block. She scribbled a shopping list for supper, swallowed a quick snack and dashed out.

Besides food purchases there was the dress. Foolish perhaps to think of it. Nothing was cheap these days and she could not see herself having many occasions to wear it. But that was not the way to look at things. Nothing had changed since Saturday when she had determined to crowd Kenneth out of her life. Tonight was the first step on the road.

"You'll buy that dress, Charlotte Lavender," she resolved. "And you'll make sure you'll wear it again. There must be some social activities here."

It was another way in which Kenneth had been right. He had made the selfsame suggestion only a few days after she had arrived. To be truthful, it appealed no more now than it had done then, but it was essential. The exquisite strain of conversations such as they had had on Sunday and again this morning could not continue. She had to find something to take her mind off this man who treated her so kindly and so humorously and so much as though she were his own small daughter.

The boutique with the red sunblinds was open and had quite a stock of maxi dresses. The one that took her fancy was a blue and white squared cotton with a square neck and short puffed sleeves. There was a flowery border of blue, mauve and lime. She was trying it on when she heard a familiar voice in the next cubicle.

"What do you think, Lou? Shall I take it?" Stephanie Wychwood—it had to be.

"Yes, definitely. It's very good." The deeper tones were similarly recogniseable. The owner was a friend of Stephanie's, Charlie had met her at the fête.

"What do you think, Samantha?" Stephanie now invited.

The rustle in the curtain was sheer temptation. "Anyone like to give *me* an opinion?" Charlie invited in her turn.

On the instant Samantha's excited face popped into view. "Oh, Charlie, it's *lovely!*" she gasped.

"What a coincidence!" Stephanie exclaimed as she pulled back the dividing curtain. She had come in to buy something for a college reunion. Samantha had a holiday from school, so she had come too.

"You know she adores clothes," Stephanie's friend whispered.

"Yes. There's a good deal of her mother in her," Stephanie agreed.

Everyone approved Charlie's selection and it was duly wrapped up. Stephanie decided to look at some other things and somewhat to Charlie's surprise Samantha elected to walk along with her to the surgery while she was waiting. She was full of yesterday's visit to the dower house. She had loved the picture of the unicorns, had helped her grandmother to water the flower garden and had come away with Jean's copy of *Anne of Green Gables*.

"Gran says she has lots more books she'll lend me," she confided. "And I'm going in to have tea with her every week. I never knew Gran was nice like that," she added seriously. "She always looks so cross. After Mummy died we used to keep away from her, 'cept at Christmas, of course. We had to go in then with Daddy to give her a present, but we never stayed long. I used to ask Daddy how soon we could get away." She paused. "Do you like Gran, Charlie? She likes you."

"I like her very much, Sam," Charlie answered truthfully. "And I think she could do with you and you with her."

The encounter had pleased her highly. She kept dwelling on it as she worked, first in the surgery and later as she put the finishing touches to the supper table.

As it was Midsummer she had chosen food that went with the season, melon, salmon mayonnaise and fresh strawberries. A simple menu, but she had been careful with the trimmings, powdered ginger, a bottle of wine, a bowl of whipped cream and some chocolate peppermints to go with the coffee. The windows were open on to the balcony and she had begged some sweet peas from Miss Roberts's garden.

As for the dress, she was pleased with it. The hot weather had tanned her neck and arms and the blue and white print emphasised it charmingly.

"Well, well," said Don appraisingly. "Not bad. Turn round. Let the dog see the rabbit."

"Allow me to inform you that I am not a rabbit," she remarked, doing so.

"We won't say what I am," he replied.

The meal went well, repaying the thought she had put into it. Don was complimentary and gay. Charlie put Kenneth out of her mind and set herself to follow suit. She even mentioned her mother's suggestion for next weekend.

"I'd love that if I were free," he said slowly. "Could we leave it open?"

Who was it this time? she wondered. Seven or eight weeks ago a reply of that sort had had terrifying implications. Now she was blessedly impervious. "As you wish," she said lightly. "Just give me a ring."

They had their coffee on the balcony. As Don had seemed to grow quieter, Charlie did most of the talking. She could not quite understand the atmosphere; from its beginning it seemed to have thickened. Don kept looking at her as though he were thinking of something else. At last she could ignore it no longer. "I hope I'm not boring you."

"Well, you do chatter, darling," he drawled. "And I confess I've never been one for the 'everyday story of country folk!' We could do something more interesting."

"What?" She was a little nonplussed.

"How about this?" He stretched an arm lazily and pulled her into its circle.

It was not the first time he had kissed her, but it was different.

"That hurts," she said uncertainly.

Don looked annoyed. He threw her a brief: "Sorry," sat up and tossed back his hair. "Well, that wasn't very successful, was it?"

"It's very hot," Charlie said lamely.

"All right, you silly kid," he returned caressingly. "No one is going to rush you. Would you fancy a drive?"

She was surprised but pleased. She loved the country in the cave of dark. Tonight there was a travelling moon and owls were hooting. Once she thought she saw one on a branch and once a harsh bark echoed across the fields.

Suddenly she had an idea. "I wonder could we find the Long Stone? It's not far from here. It walks on Mid-summer Eve."

"What are you talking about?" Don sighed.

"It's just a legend, of course," Charlie said, explaining. "But . . ."

"But you'd like to see it. What a child you are! Coming out to gaze at a rotten old stone," he grumbled. "Well, see if you can spot a sign. I suppose there'll be one, if it exists at all." The last words were said under his breath. She had not been meant to hear them.

More and more it made her realise that they were poles apart.

There was no sign to Hopehampton's piece of history and Don's patience was soon exhausted. "It's probably somewhere over there," he said finally. "I can't go any closer. If you want to, you're on your own."

The wall was low, the land was pasture and across in the distance a high boulder, like a giant millstone, cast a shadow on the ground.

"That must be it. Perhaps it will come to meet me," Charlie joked as she got out.

It struck her that she must cut an old-fashioned figure, flitting across the grass in her long skirt. One of the Brontë sisters? No, the setting was not bleak enough for Haworth. It was eerie, though, and this, she remembered, was also St. John's Eve when bonfires used to blaze through pagan Europe and still did, so she had read, in some remote parts of the country. "Supposing I were to see something," she thought, and stopped in her tracks. It was not that the witches had suddenly appeared, it was the memory of that morning's talk with Kenneth.

He had been so insistent and she had forgotten so soon.

Walking stone or not, she had made a promise and must

keep it. She turned to go back to the car and in the same moment a form dodged out from behind the Long Stone. "You're seeing things," Charlie told herself. Her heart had missed a beat. She looked back and it was gone, walked on a pace and turned and it was there again, a small dark shape, barely perceptible, crouching against the stone.

"If I'd gone on . . . " she thought.

She had never been even close to it, but the prospect was unnerving. Peeping Tom—or worse—something was waiting by the Long Stone on Midsummer Eve.

"What's up? Did you get cold feet?" Don teased.

"I suppose I did. There was someone there already. I wasn't sure what they were doing." It was interesting that the possibility of danger had patently not occurred to him.

"Oh well," he said indifferently. "What's there to see anyway? Let's go."

Charlie closed the car door and sat back. She wished she had something to put over her shoulders, for all at once there seemed to have been a drop in temperature. Yes, she had cold feet and coldness in the pit of her stomach. It could not have been a hobgoblin—had she ever seriously thought so—and it mightn't have been the Peeping Tom. In any case, surely it had been too small, and if it wasn't . . . then what was any small person up to, out there alone at past eleven—*unless something had happened to them.*

"Turn right, Don," she said firmly, drawing a breath. "I want to pass it again. I think that may have been a child and it could be lost."

The road skirted the field and was plainly the correct route for viewing the stone. There was a gate and the boulder was only a few yards inside it. And yes, as anticipated, a figure was standing uncertainly on the verge.

"I was right, it is a child," Charlie thought, peering forward. Quite a tall child—or was that only the capsule like shape of jeans and anorak? Boy or girl? Boy, she decided; no hair appeared to be showing.

"Can we help you?" she called as Don slowed up. "Should you be out by yourself?"

The child turned its face away and then thought better of it. In the same moment Charlie realised that it was a girl with her hair tucked into her collar and that she was crying.

"Are you all right?" Charlie called, snapping open the door.

Next instant, and speechless with astonishment, she found herself staring at a tear-blotched but familiar face.

"Don't tell Daddy," the face's owner said urgently. "Oh, please, Charlie, don't let Daddy know. I can't find Brenda's bicycle."

Samantha had been in the wars. She had grazed both knees and one elbow and had sore-looking friction burns on her hands. She was also incoherent. Charlie got the story at last.

Kenneth had promised to take her to the Long Stone and had been prevented by an emergency call. He had asked Stephanie to baby-sit. No one, it seemed, had taken any notice of Samantha's prior claim. She had had to go to the Long Stone, she now repeated vigorously, and it had had to be tonight because Martha said this was the best time. Daddy had been hateful, he didn't care about her, and she had told him so.

Passing over the disclosure that old Martha, the apparent mute, had spoken, Charlie went on to discover that Samantha had sneaked out of the house via her bedroom window, a sloping roof and the drainpipe. She had then helped herself to friend Brenda's bicycle which she knew was never taken indoors at night. So far so good, but not far from her goal she had ridden into a crater in the road and had come a cropper. When she had picked up the bicycle "it wouldn't go", so there had been nothing to do but leave it and proceed on foot to the Long Stone. Sadly when she had returned to retrieve the casualty it was no longer there. For the past while she had searched frantically, even retracing her steps to see if somehow "it could have got to the Long Stone." But no, Brenda's bicycle had vanished. Samantha was beside herself. Once started on her tale of woe, she could not stop crying. Charlie was afraid she would make herself ill.

She had no doubt that Kenneth would be angry, but when she telephoned him his voice was so quiet as to be unfamiliar.

"They weren't alone. I never leave them alone. I don't

see how she got out."

For the first time in their relationship, Charlie felt the older. No man cared more for his children, few fought so hard against odds. This must be a body blow.

"I know how this must seem," she said gently. "I know it's shattering, but she's quite safe. Actually she's in bed. She was dead beat."

In this she had used her initiative. To confront Samantha with her justifiably irate father in her present state would have been courting disaster. Ignoring Don's disgust, she had brought the child back to the flat, cleaned up her cuts and grazes, soothed her as best she could and tucked her into bed. An edgy comment from Don about 'idiot children leaving bicycles in the middle of the road where they could cause a car crash' had helped her to elicit over a cup of cocoa that this was precisely what Samantha had done. It also suggested that the patrol car could have taken it into custody. "We'll find it, darling, don't worry," she had comforted. "And Daddy won't be one bit cross when he understands." It was more than she herself had done at that moment.

"Oh, crumbs," said Kenneth dejectedly. The funny little expletive went to her heart. "Why do we tell them *anything*? I'll keep my mouth shut in future."

"You told Sam something?"

"Yes, yes," he sighed. "I told her about the stone. There's an old superstition about the holes in it. If you had a bad arm or leg and passed it through one of the apertures it was supposed to be a cure. So nothing would do Sam but to take her voice to the Long Stone—and I hope for its own sake," he added forcibly, "it didn't ask her to sing!"

It was a comical situation, not only because of Samantha but because her erudite father had been hoist with his own petard. He could be so scathing about foolishness and yet he had been persuaded to pander to it.

Charlie found herself dangerously between laughter and tears.

"She said *you* had promised to take her."

"I did. I must have been mad."

Charlie did not think so. She was thrilled to think he could be foolish and irrational like herself. "Don't be cross," she said softly. "I know how you feel, but look past her disobedience if you can. Think what it means to her and what she's been through. Her poor little hands are all burned from the drainpipe and she hasn't said one word about them or her cut knees. Please, Ken, make allowances."

"You would, I know," he said unexpectedly. "I shall have to try. I'm very grateful, Charles. I mean that."

Don looked up as she returned to the sitting-room. She tried not to see how ill-humoured his expression had become. "Is he coming over?"

"He can't. Jason might wake." Kenneth's responsibilities must weight heavily at times, she thought compassionately. As it was, Samantha would have to be fetched early next morning in order to get her home, changed for school and ferried off again to catch the bus. The fact that he was also due to put Hannibal down would not help.

"He asks for it," Don said irritably. "Why doesn't he get another woman? Pick her for the kids and the house, he can have his fun on the side."

"I hope you're joking." Charlie kept cool with an effort.

"Should I be? It's 1975," he returned. "And to me it makes a lot of sense. If I were Kenneth Carr I'd look round for someone like you who would obviously drool over my children and never say bo to me. And then you could all live happily after, you, Carr and Jasmine."

"That's a revolting thing to say!" Charlie raged. "Kenneth would never . . ."

"I know. Keep your hair on," he drawled. "I know he wouldn't. I know more than you do, as it happens. Jasmine got pretty confidential last night. He's one marriage to the bad already and he still hasn't learned to compromise. It's all or nothing, I gather, more fool he!"

"Let's not discuss it," Charlie said tightly.

It did not surprise her that Jasmine had laid her cards on the table. She and Don had the same code of ethics. Jasmine would call it 'frank' to explain where she stood with Kenneth. Charlie was old-fashioned, it made her shudder. If Kenneth's marriage had been unhappy it seemed the height of bad taste to talk about it with Don so early in their acquaintance. He had said 'last night', but she took that for a slip of the tongue. Last night he had been at home celebrating his parents' anniversary.

"I can be frank too, I don't like Don any more," she thought. Even silently, it was a relief to own it.

The window was still open and the clock in the church tower struck midnight.

"My goodness," Charlie said uncertainly, "it's late. Don, I'm sorry about this. I know it wasn't the evening we planned."

"You can say that again," he grinned lazily. "But better late than never. Come and sit down."

At least he no longer looked angry. She sat down, stifling a yawn which would surely have been the last insult. He fondled her hand and stroked the inside of her wrist. "Kiss me, Charlotte. Kiss me properly."

A row had to be avoided, but other considerations were at stake.

"Just once, then, to say goodnight," she firmed her voice. "How long will it take you to get home?"

There was an amused silence. "That sounds a bit inhospitable," he murmured. "This, after all, is on my way to London."

"I have no room," Charlie fenced. "Samantha's in the spare bed."

"Not quite what I had in mind," Don remarked.

It was absurd to feel like apologising. She set her chin. "I'm sorry, Don, it's not on."

His face clouded. "You're burying your head in the sand, girl. I agree you'd make a wonderful mother for Kenneth Carr's children, but, like I told you, he's got to fancy the bird."

Charlie all but stamped. "Will you stop talking about Kenneth! His affairs are his own, so are mine. I've said no and I mean it. Please go before I lose my temper."

"*Before?*" he echoed, chuckling. "You could have fooled me. All right." He stood up. "But seriously, Charlotte, I think you're making a mistake. We may not have a future, you and I, but we can give each other pleasure—I guarantee it. So why not?" He took her chin caressingly in his hand. Reconsider?"

She shook her head.

"Oh well." He showed her the palms of his hands. "If the lady won't, the lady won't. Pity we found that child. She's so exactly like her father. You started thinking about him."

"As a matter of fact Samantha takes after her mother," Charlie said coldly.

"I hope not," Don quipped from the door. "Jasmine says she drank like a fish."

Charlie's head spun. It was horror upon anger upon shock. Her thoughts were pistol shots. Kenneth facing *that*. Jean watching her daughter. Samantha perhaps old enough to be affected. And Jasmine *gossiping* about it. Don found it diverting—she could see that. Interesting, even chuckle-raising, nothing more.

Don wasn't the worst offender, but he was near to her. She took up her hand and slapped him across the face.

They were staring at each other each equally astonished when the door opened slightly, a voice said: "Charles, are you there?" and Kenneth, wooden-faced, stood looking at them.

There was no doubt he had sensed the atmosphere. "I beg your pardon. I knocked, but you didn't hear me. As I saw you were still up I used my key."

His eyes were bland. She told herself that half past midnight was not an excessively late hour and yet she felt as if the situation with Don was blazoned on the walls of the room. "You said you couldn't come..." It was a guilty-sounding statement.

Kenneth apologised for the intrusion. An opportunity had presented itself. He had an eiderdown over his arm and Charlie noticed that he was wearing slippers. It did indeed imply that he had come on the impulse.

"You're not intruding." She had a miserable feeling that he had stressed the word. "Don was just going."

Here at least there were no complications. Don said the briefest of farewells and got into his car. By mutual consent the projected meeting next weekend was not mentioned. Charlie closed the door and went back to the sitting-room.

It was ridiculous to be daunted by a look, but Kenneth's was quellingly direct. She knew he was displeased and would not be chary of saying so. Their positions, reversed for a short while on the telephone, were back to what they had always been.

"I know you told me you weren't born yesterday," he observed. "But having met your mother, I feel a certain amount of responsibility . . ."

It was a tactless approach. "For what?" Charlie struck in, her colour rising. "Not for me, please. Mummy will let you off the hook."

He ignored the gibe. "I was going to say for seeing that your habitual warmheartedness is not imposed on."

"It wasn't and it wouldn't have been." She was angry. Need he sound so pompous and domineering?

"In a sense it already has. You have a working day tomorrow and you need your sleep."

"Good gracious!" Raw nerves put her at pressure. "One late night. How often does that happen?"

"How should I know?" he cornered reasonably. "Now let's change the subject. I thought I should get Sam home tonight, if she's so tired she probably won't wake. It's true I didn't think I could manage it, Steph is an early bird, but Jean sleeps badly and goes to bed very late. There was a light in her sitting-room, so I rang her. She agreed to stay with Jason till we got back. Which means I mustn't delay."

"Of course." Charlie stood back feeling superfluous. "Well, you know the way." Things in Woodsgift seemed to be moving fast. "What did Jean think about Samantha?" she added curiously.

"I got the distinct impression she was on her side," Kenneth confided. "Yes, I . . ." he hesitated. "I suddenly felt I should have Sam at home. Not that you haven't been extraordinarily kind and not that I'm unappreciative. Does that make a mite of sense? I suppose not."

Drat the man! One minute he lectured you, the next he touched your heart. He had wanted to make peace with Samantha so much that he had literally come out in slippers to get her.

"It makes a lot of sense," Charlie said softly. "I'm sure you're right."

"I'm sure you were too in what you said," he returned unexpectedly. His hand went to her arm and squeezed it.

158

"Thanks again."

Charlie had not intended to peep, but when he went into the spare room he left the door open. Samantha blinked into wakefulness and saw him. The look on her face was enough. "Daddy!" She struggled up and Kenneth's arms went round her in a bear hug of reassurance.

"It's all right, it's all right, Sam," he comforted. "I'm sorry too."

CHAPTER TWELVE

IF Midsummer Eve had been a peak of darkness, Midsummer Day was back to normal. The spectre of Kenneth's marriage which had haunted Charlie's dreams seemed smaller when she saw her boss get out of the estate car and stride across the yard looking just as usual.

"That's done," he said briefly, referring to the horse he had put down. Jean had asked him not to perform the task at Woodsgift so Hannibal had been driven over to the hunt kennels. The old horse's happiest days had been spent with hounds, even today he had become pleased and excited when he heard them.

"Who took him?" Charlie asked.

"I drove. Jean came with me. Guy had services." She guessed that this had not been arranged by chance. An enquiry about Samantha brought a terse: "Fine, thanks. The police have the bicycle. They were looking for the body!"

So all was well that ended well. Charlie went back to reception, took a few phone calls and received the first patient, a tabby cat who had tangled with a trap on Sunday night and had a badly torn mouth and tongue. It was his second visit, he would need several more shots of antibiotics before he could begin to eat again, but Kenneth was hopeful that he need not be put down.

She took the cat's card into the surgery. "Oh yes," said Kenneth. "Anyone else?"

There wasn't.

"She won't mind waiting a minute. Close the door." He looked at Charlie consideringly. "There's something you should think about. You may feel it's not my business. I'm not sure it is. But—you're friendly with Don Harris. Do you know if he knew Jasmine before last Saturday?"

"He didn't." Charlie shook her head. "I introduced them."

"Yes," Kenneth folded his lips, "that's what I thought.

I—suspect they spent the rest of the weekend together."

Charlie was silent. His meaning was plain. Don had told her he had family commitments for Sunday, but he had made that slip about Jasmine saying something to him 'last night'. She was not in the least surprised. On Saturday their attraction to each other had been obvious.

"I . . ." Suddenly Kenneth's side of it flashed into her mind. If he had been battling to persuade Jasmine to marry him this news would be comfortless. "I think we should give them the benefit of the doubt," she said quickly. "Don told me he had to spend Sunday with his people."

"In other words you'd rather I hadn't spoken?"

"No, I . . . well, just what I said," Charlie mumbled.

"All right." He gestured. "Now that cat. Bring him in, please, and his owner. I've noticed he's better when she holds him." It was dismissal. She could tell by the tone of his voice that he was put out.

Jean Wychwood telephoned just as she was locking up. It was to suggest that as Sunday's afternoon tea had been disrupted, Charlie should come round for supper. "The company will cheer Guy up." In the circumstances a refusal would have been unfeeling. Charlie asked that Guy should not trouble to call for her, gave Nicky the run he had missed yesterday and set out. She had gone only a short distance when a car drew up. Its horn hooted and Stephanie beckoned her in. "You look as if you're going my way!

"I must congratulate you," she added as they drove on. "You've worked a miracle between Jean and Samantha. I don't know how you did it. It's something I've been attempting for years."

Charlie said shortly that it had been no miracle. She had merely made a suggestion on the spur of the moment.

"Ah yes, but the miracle was you'd already got Jean to like you," Stephanie remarked. "Poor Jean, I'm afraid she became very withdrawn after Marjorie's death. It was very sad, of course, coming when it did."

Charlie waited. It seemed a pregnant moment.

"I don't like gossiping, but perhaps this is more in the nature of friendly guidance," her companion went on.

"Marjorie was—ill when she married. For years I had no suspicion, of course I was teaching then and didn't see much of her. She was repressed at home, that may have had something to do with it, and Jean had ambitious plans for her marriage. Marjorie wanted to marry Kenneth, but this was actively discouraged, and then quite suddenly the veto was lifted and much to everyone's surprise the engagement was on and they were being urged not to delay."

In the pause a sickening suspicion dawned. "You're not implying that Jean *knew* . . ." Charlie began, and stopped.

"She had discovered, yes," Stephanie answered. "And she thought that if she withdrew her opposition and got Marjorie happily married everything would be all right. Needless to say it was not as simple as that. Marjorie needed professional help, poor girl. It was a tragedy."

"But Kenneth . . ." Again Charlie paused. She was afraid that her involuntary lingering on the name would betray her.

"Kenneth realised, of course, though not immediately. Marjorie did try, and there's no doubt she adored him. She was like Guy, you see, young in her ways and needing someone to lean on. It was at its worst when Samantha was two or three. There was one deradful occasion when Marjorie took the child down to the lake and allowed her to go too near the edge and she fell in. I know it's not deep, but Samantha was only a toddler and if Kenneth hadn't just happened along she could have drowned. That brought matters to a head and Marjorie consented at last to go away for treatment. It was a long business, but in the end she did seem to improve. Things got better and she set her heart on a second child, but as you know her health wasn't up to it and she died when Jason was born."

"Oh, it's so sad," Charlie said pitifully. "Oh, Stephanie, *why*? Why, when he'd gone through so much?" She was giving herself away, but she couldn't help it. The words came bubbling.

Now all was plain. What Jean had meant by referring to the marriage as having crucified him. What Kenneth himself had meant by his mother-in-law's gift for seizing the moment. And why he had now turned to Jasmine, attractive, but more than that, strong. Someone who would never

162

lean.

"Do you think Jasmine will ever marry him?" Again it was an artless question and Stephanie's look of surprise was blushmaking.

"You think it rests with Jasmine?" the older woman questioned. "Do you like her?"

"Not all the time," Charlie said honestly. "But then I don't have her conflicts. And look how lovely she is. That matters. Oh yes, I do think they'll marry eventually. Don't you?"

"Maybe. I daresay you know the signs better than I do. As I once told you, I'm not 'with it' any more. But no one really knows what Kenneth thinks. He can be very close. Jasmine is not altogether my style, but I know she's attractive and he'd have a lot to gain financially if he married her. I often think, though, that he won't remarry. He's had enough to scare him off, heaven knows."

It had been a sad conversation. Charlie had to make an effort to throw off her mood of depression when she was dropped at the dower house, but at least Guy, when he came in from a parish meeting, was in better spirits than she had anticipated.

"I've asked Kenneth to drop in," Jean volunteered over supper. "I think it would be a good idea to replace poor Hannibal and he happens to know someone who has a hunter for sale." Recent events and especially Stephanie's disclosures had sharpened Charlie's wits. A new horse could be one way of keeping Guy at home. She sighed for Jean and for Guy who seemed eternally shackled by his own good nature.

One person, however, for whom there seemed no need to sigh was Samantha. A few minutes later she came up the drive with Kenneth and Max. She was skipping along, her hair out of sight under a canvas hat and her tongue going ninety to the dozen.

"She has such gaiety," Charlie thought tenderly. It was miraculous that this child sparkling with imagination should have developed from the baby of those sad times. There were many possibilities for Samantha in years to come and one certainty. She would find love.

Conceivably Kenneth had taken last night to heart. So

often any extra particle of spare time was Jason's prerogative, but this evening it had been given to Samantha. As he made to part from her at the Dower House Jean went out. Charlie heard her say: "Oh, nonsense. Five minutes won't hurt her," and next instant Samantha had skipped into the kitchen and was helping to set out glasses on a tray.

"I'm sorry I can't take my hat off," she explained. "If I do, my hair will fall down. Do you like it up, Charlie? It's an experiment."

Charlie had felt privileged when Jean had accepted her offer to bring in the drinks and all through the evening she found herself included in whatever came up for discussion.

"Charlie agrees we should look that horse over," Jean said amiably. "Perhaps you could spare her one afternoon when Guy is free."

It was flattering but unmerited. "I'm afraid I'd just be a passenger, Jean," Charlie said quickly. "I wouldn't know what to look for."

"We'd like to have you anyway," her hostess assured. "One of these days we'll have to get you up. Kenneth, is this horse a suitable ride for a beginner?"

"I believe so," Kenneth said distantly. It was plain the suggestion of time off had not found favour and Charlie did not blame him. She would put things right tomorrow.

Meantime, Samantha was very funny in this her debut at a grown-up gathering. She sipped her lemonade, nibbled crisps and made conversation.

"How would you like to meet one of those things in your garden?" she asked Charlie, and pointed at the cavorting unicorns in the picture.

"Very much indeed," Charlie returned. "If I had a garden!"

Samantha looked wise. "Have they got them at the Cotswold Farm Park? I can't remember. When we went there was such a lot to see."

"Ask Daddy," Charlie suggested. She was concerned about Kenneth upon whom a cloud seemed to have settled. It was in sad contrast to the smile he had worn coming up the drive with Samantha. Alas, the attempt to rouse him was vain. He gave his daughter a brusque negative and did not pursue the subject.

Samantha was undeterred. "I expect you'd have to get them from China. That's where the London Zoo got the pandas."

"Now, Sam, on your feet," Kenneth interrupted at this point. "If you go on at this pace you'll never be up for school in the morning."

In a strange way the room seemed to lose something as Samantha left it. For Charlie, with the image of Marjorie Carr in mind, the child was a clear blend of youthful appeal and old-world manners. She herself had received a kiss and a most touching farewell speech.

"Thanks for looking after me last night. Someday I'll pay you for it. Daddy says you were extraordinarily kind."

Jean was also kissed and seemed very pleased. "Good-night, Sam. And come again soon. We have a lot to do before Sunday.

"I've had an idea about Samantha," she announced when the child had gone. "Obviously she needs more of the limelight. I've prevailed upon Guy to talk to the vicar and the upshot is that next Sunday she's going to read the lesson. It's a pilot scheme. If it's successful there'll be other occasions."

It was an inspiration. Charlie gazed at her hostess in undisguised admiration. There was certainly no denying Jean Wychwood's forcefulness. Once her interest was engaged she got results.

Samantha was to be personally tutored in the Dower House and Guy was giving her the necessary rehearsal in the church. It was to be a surprise for Kenneth, kept secret until the last minute. "Tell him in the car, I should think," Guy suggested. "Otherwise he probably wouldn't face it!"

Guy had certainly taken his loss well. Charlie suspected, somewhat disquietingly, that her own presence had helped the situation.

When the time came for her to take her leave he humoured her desire to walk home. They took the path through the woods past the spot where on her first Sunday Samantha had pointed out the fox's lair. It was very dark under the canopy of trees, a capsule-like blackness, grey burnt at the edges.

"I love walking in the woods," Charlie observed. "Kenneth made me promise not to if I were alone."

"I know. He told me about the man he saw," Guy agreed. "But you're not alone now." His arm tightened protectively. A moment later came the question she had been dreading. "Charlie, you do know, don't you, you could always have me?"

She wished she need not answer, but to hedge would be unfair.

"I know that's the nicest thing anyone has ever said to me."

"But you're not going to take me up on it?" As she did not immediately reply, he went on honestly: "All right, don't say anything. I know when I've backed a loser."

"I know too," Charlie thought ruefully.

"Must we talk about it?" she queried. "I hope you also know how much I value your friendship. Let's leave it at that."

The week went on. For the first time since she had come to Hopehampton the days had a leaden feel. She wondered if Kenneth was brooding over Jasmine's friendship with Don. He had not referred to it again, but ever since the evening at the Dower House he had seemed preoccupied and short in manner. Unprecedented in Charlie's experience was an exchange one morning with a middle-aged cat owner who reproached him for refusing her a house call. "Your grandfather would never have asked me to carry that great heavy basket all the way down here."

"There's a remedy for that," Kenneth commented. "The cat is grossly overweight."

Charlie had felt apprehensive for the caller who had arrived panting heavily. "She almost had a heart attack," she said afterwards. "It scared me."

"As it was meant to," he retorted. "The lady is noted for it. And for not paying her bills. We, however, are running a practice, not a charitable institution. And, by the way, neither are we running it for fun. I'm afraid you must arrange your jaunts with Guy and Jean for when you're off duty."

"I meant to say that." She was vexed with herself for

not having done so before. "I wouldn't dream of anything else. I've already told Guy so."

"Oh?" He looked at her sharply and obviously gratified. "I see. I was premature. All right, let's push on."

The old Kenneth with his teasing comments on her grammar seemed to have vanished for all time. These days the only common ground they had was work. The change in him could only be due to his wretchedness over Don and Jasmine and for that Charlie knew she must assign some blame to herself. Don would never have come to Hopehampton if she had not been there.

On Saturday she bumped into Jasmine in the greengrocer's and was surprised at the friendliness of her greeting. For the first time ever the irksome 'Mouse' seemed to hold more warmth than condescension.

"I suppose you're chasing back to that dog," Jasmine added teasingly. "Have you time for a coffee?"

An astonished Charlie agreed, hoping her hesitancy did not show. There was no denying, however, that Jasmine was in a different and much more likeable mood. And was it imagination—or just the dark bronze of her suntan—that her features had a leaner, more sculptured look? Charlie had sometimes thought the same about her own. It came when you were unhappy—or unsure.

"Look, mouse, I owe you an apology," Jasmine said abruptly. "May as well get it over with. It won't be news to you. I did undo Nicky's collar on Saturday—I thought it would be amusing. I was sorry afterwards and I've told Ken so."

There was little to say. Charlie had never expected capitulation. Now that it had come she felt strangely compassionate.

"That was nice of you," she said gently. "Thanks."

"Oh, I'm not a nice person," Jasmine corrected. "I think I told you once that what I have I hold. The trouble is I . . ." She dug the spoon into the bowl of brown sugar. "Perhaps I'm getting old."

It was so ludicrous that Charlie laughed.

"Ah-ha!" Jasmine was still prodding the sugar. "He's a Peter Pan, isn't he? Can he cry?"

"You're talking about Don," Charlie said quietly. "No,

I don't think so. Not yet. I suppose he will some day. I suppose that comes to us all."

She watched the long brown fingers grasp the spoon handle. "Kenneth is hers for the asking," she thought dully. "And she wants Don."

"You're wiser than I gave you credit for, mouse," Jasmine remarked softly. "I don't know whether to bless you or curse you for bringing him here."

Charlie drew a breath. She could hardly believe that she was being asked for advice and at the same time she could not turn aside. From either this new Jasmine—or from Kenneth.

"Forget Don," she said jerkily. "Pretend you don't see him and he'll go away."

"You know, I might just do that," Jasmine answered thoughtfully. "I might just do that, mouse, once and for all."

Something told Charlie as she hurried up the hilly street that a decision had been reached. Stephanie would view it with reserve, Jean with abhorrence. It could jeopardise Samantha's new-found relationship with her grandmother and that would be a tragedy. But a minor one, Charlie argued, compared with what it could do for the man who had waited so patiently.

She was rounding the corner by the hairdresser's when she was again hailed, this time by a childish and very excited voice. "Charlie!" Samantha called. "Do you know where I'm going?"

Behind her hovered Jean's tall figure.

"Guess!" Samantha encouraged. "I'll give you a hint. The next time you see me you may not recognise me."

Charlie thought that was unlikely. Jean said tartly that she hoped it was not. "Kenneth has let this child's hair get in a terrible state."

Together they went into the hairdresser's tiny hall, Samantha popping out again to confide in a thrilled whisper: "If you're in church tomorrow I'll be the one in the long dress."

"Oh, Sam!" Charlie was at a loss for words. So much to happen to one little girl in the space of a few days—a long dress, a hair-do, an office to fulfil. And such a pity that she herself was going home for the day. She said so and Samantha's face dropped.

"Oh, Charlie, you can't! I want you. You must be there."

"You'll have plenty of others, darling, Daddy and Jason and Gran and Stephanie and Jasmine."

"I want you," Samantha protested.

And I want to be there, Charlie acknowledged. Well, why not? The visit home would only have been for a few hours and she knew her mother would understand if she postponed it.

The morning was fine with a pale blue feathered sky. Her fourth Sunday in Hopehampton, Charlie calculated, and the only one to date on which she had not been invited to Woodsgift in the afternoon. Not that she was complaining about that. The premonition that she would soon hear news about Kenneth and Jasmine could not be stifled. She could be glad of it for Kenneth's sake, but coming into contact with him socially would stir up the kind of thoughts that did one no good.

"You and I will go for a long walk," she promised Nicky.

Some chemistry about the church bells, now echoing round the four corners of the yard, made it impossible to feel downhearted. She gave a last flick to her hair, slung on her shoulder bag and hurried off. As she came to the lych gate Stephanie was parking her car and immediately asked her to lunch.

"If I said I had a previous engagement with a dog would you think me awful?" Charlie was not dressed for going out.

"I'd think we could get over that," Stephanie returned. "After church we'll go and call for him."

So that was that. "I can't hurt her feelings," Charlie decided, and accepted.

In church it seemed that intuition had been right. Up the aisle together walked Jasmine, Kenneth and Jason. Jasmine looked composed and a little paler than usual. A dark large-brimmed hat was perched on the back of her head. It was a piquant thought that someone with such a wonderful future should not be radiating happiness. But at that moment Charlie had no time for introspection because Guy had just brought Samantha to the lectern to find out the place, and Samantha was *gorgeous*.

It was true, she *was* almost unrecognisable. The hair that had been cut and shaped to fall like a bell not only looked silkier but had new lights in it. The full-length dress was Victorian. Its flowers of rose and turquoise went into a different print on hem and collar.

"Good gracious, it might be Marjorie!" Stephanie's whisper confirmed Charlie's own feeling. In the gospel according to her grandmother God never closed one door without opening another. Jean Wychwood, she fancied, had today found a new purpose in living. Certainly the look on her face as Samantha read quite beautifully the story of the sacrifice of Isaac was good to see.

Charlie did not claim to be psychic. Only once on the road to the Devil's Churchyard that other Sunday morning had she sensed something in the air. Then it had seemed menacing, like a premonition of evil. Today, quite suddenly, as Samantha voiced Abraham's words: 'My son, God will provide himself a lamb for a burnt offering,' it came again.

Nonsense, of course. In fact a tribute to the reader who obviously had both her father's love of words and the power to use them.

"And what happened the last time you felt spooky?" Charlie reminded herself. "Absolutely nothing."

In the churchyard, Samantha's beam as people congratulated her was heartwarming. Kenneth too looked as pleased as Punch. "She didn't do badly, did she?" he asked as Charlie came up.

It was Samantha's hour of glory, but it was shortlived. A man had pushed through the gathering to touch Kenneth on the arm. He turned with an exclamation of surprise and they spoke together. Charlie, scanning the two serious faces, deduced correctly that her employer's professional services were being sought.

In confirmation came Stephanie's voice beside her: "Something must be wrong. That's Mr. Marshall's farm manager."

Charlie knew Mr. Marshall by repute. He was Kenneth's

biggest client, a wealthy landowner and breeder with a herd of prize cattle. He lived about twenty-five miles from Hopehampton, but his connection with the practice spanned several generations. A call from Marshall's End amounted to a royal command, especially since they had been ringing Woodsgift unsuccessfully, and the manager's decision to drive over and look for him had been a last desperate measure.

"Right. If you like to go ahead I'll be on your tail." Kenneth came back to the group looking rueful. He had hoped they would all come back to the house for a drink; now the pleasure would have to be postponed.

His words broke up the party. Jean, who had been chatting to her grandchildren, moved towards her own car as Jasmine hustled them into hers. Kenneth in the blue estate car had already shot down the road.

"He's going so fast it must be something serious," Stephanie observed as she and Charlie followed suit. "I hope it's not the bull that took all the prizes last year."

As always Nicky was glad to go to Woodsgift and Bobby in the role of host was obviously just as glad to see him. Stephanie suggested that Charlie should take them both 'round the block' while she put lunch in the oven.

It was delightful understatement. Charlie with Nicky's leash firmly grasped went down the sloping main drive, took the footpath into the woods and, mindful of instructions, did not penetrate further than the point where it joined with the back avenue running from the Manor. Here she took the home branch and came out on the lawn where Samantha and Jason were chasing each other.

It was a domestic scene. A radio was playing on the grass and Jasmine was hosing the flowerbeds. Charlie, endeavouring to skirt the garden unobtrusively, was hailed and again Jasmine proved friendly and talkative. No more was said on yesterday's topic, but the signs that she was determinedly cooling her fever for Don were everywhere.

Charlie was about to leave when the telephone in the sitting-room started ringing. Jasmine, who had dashed through the french door to answer it, waved at her to turn down the radio. There was something about the gesture that suggested more than normal irritation. A bad line,

Charlie supposed as she complied, or someone important.

It had been a desultory thought, but suddenly it attained import. Jasmine had not closed the door, her voice was audible, rising, excited, intense. Her words were guarded, her phrases terse. "Yes, I could ... oh, I don't know ... should I ... three hours barring hold-ups ... all right you're on ..."

When she came back to the garden it was impossible not to notice the change in her. Her cheeks were flushed, her hair seemed uncannily blacker and more luxuriant. She tossed it back like a colt.

"How long will Ken be? You should know, mouse."

One couldn't hazard. Charlie said so.

"It's just that ... oh, never mind. I'll ask Steph."

The name rang a bell for Samantha. She came running over. "Can we go now, Jasmine? Steph's home. She'll take Jay."

Whatever was in prospect, it was unwelcome. Jasmine's eyes narrowed giving her face a pinched look. "God, I forgot. I can't, Sam, not now. Something's just come up."

Something, Charlie questioned, or *someone*? It would be tragic if Jasmine's resolve were to be so frail.

"You promised," Samantha accused. "You did, Jasmine. You promised me first!"

"Oh, shut up, let me think," Jasmine flashed.

Plainly she had promised to take Samantha somewhere and now wanted to opt out. "That telephone call," Charlie thought suspiciously. *"That telephone call came from Don."*

It was incredible that Jasmine should hesitate. Send him packing, Charlie willed silently, he won't mean it, he's not for keeps. But the underlying thought which she had had from the beginning remained. Here were two of a kind, tough, ruthless and communicating. It was like a Greek tragedy, dreadful but inexorable.

"Could I take Samantha wherever it is she wants to go?" she suggested.

It was the wrong move. Samantha's face became convulsed.

"No!" she bawled. "Not you, Charlie, you can't!"

"Be quiet!" Jasmine clapped her hands to her ears. She

172

looked at her watch. "I suppose I did promise. All right, let's see if Steph will have Jason. You too, probably, if your dad's not here when we get back. And you'll have to be quick, mind. I've very little time."

The drift of this was surprising, since Charlie had visualised Ken and the children having already been invited to lunch at the Manor. Obviously not, and for her own part a case of the ill wind. Jason's company was always diverting.

"There's a note for Ken on the door," Jasmine explained, handing her small charge over. "And if he shouldn't be back by the time Samantha and I get home perhaps you'd have her too. Sorry to trouble you like this, Stephanie, but I've just had a phone call from an old friend."

"That's perfectly all right." Stephanie, always hospitable, saw no problem.

Charlie kept her own counsel and took Jason into the garden. He, however, had the wanderlust. He knew that the land behind Stephanie's hedge belonged to his grandmother. Somewhat wilfully he insisted on squeezing through and when at last Charlie succeeded in marching him up the slope to the main drive, he wriggled from her grasp and darted through the gate on to his own lawn. Max was there and came bounding to meet them with a swish of his tail.

"I wish we could be friends, Max," Charlie thought. Kenneth would say she was being absurd, but she had never been sure that the dog did not despise her.

Nicky's wild welcome from his look-out on Stephanie's terrace made her feel emotional. It was not the first time and it was silly, but whatever the beagle lacked in obedience he made up for in heart.

"Quiet, you silly dog," she said affectionately.

It was not his fault that he aroused such depressing link-ups. Noble, disciplined Max so aptly matched his master. Kenneth ridiculed Nicky. "He finds me a joke too," Charlie thought achingly.

She lifted aside the barrier which confined Nicky and Bobby and shepherded Jason on to the terrace. As he ran ahead stamping his feet, Stephanie came out of the house: "Lunch is ready. I was just going to call. Haven't you brought Samantha?"

"No. Should we have? Are they back?" Charlie asked.

"That's the puzzle. Jasmine is. The car went past five minutes ago. Didn't you see it?"

Charlie shook her head. "There's no sign of Sam out there. And Kenneth is not back. We've just been in the garden with Max. How odd, Stephanie. Jasmine couldn't possibly have come back alone."

"Come back from where?" Stephanie cornered. They looked at each other.

"We don't know, do we?" the older woman challenged. "And Jasmine is quite unpredictable. I'm never happy about her taking charge of the children. I've said this to you before, she could turn round and leave them *anywhere*, if she wanted to do something else."

"Oh no!" Charlie was horrified. "Oh no, surely she couldn't."

Who could be so irresponsible? She echoed the question silently. It had an unreassuring effect. She saw the nervous toss of Jasmine's dark head and the way her face had suddenly grown thin. Thin, she now thought, with a sad desperate desire. In that frame of mind Jasmine was *not* responsible. She would certainly tolerate no opposition to her own need.

The question was—had she met opposition, because Samantha in the mood in which she had set out, strung up, noisy and exhilarated, had seemed almost fey.

"I'm going to find out," Charlie clipped, and ran.

Jasmine was home and had changed into a long cotton dress, its pattern slashed across like the bars of a portcullis. A black lacy garment which could have been shawl or waistcoat hung over one arm. Oh yes, she said casually, quite true, Samantha was following. When Charlie enquired from where she grew vague. The whole silly business was supposed to be a secret. The child had had a notion about something she wanted to find.

"Did you leave her?" Charlie demanded.

"Well, in a way." Jasmine shrugged. "I gave her fair warning. 'Be back at the car in ten minutes or else I'll go without you'. As a matter of fact I waited fifteen. And now, mouse, if you'll stand out of the way, I must run."

It was appalling. In seconds—and quite airily—Jasmine was capable of doing just that. "Hold on," Charlie flashed, gripping her arm. "Where was this? You must know."

The directions she got were disquieting. Into the town, Jasmine said, and then right and a left fork, near a footpath sign. That was where she had waited. Samantha had sloped off across country. The car could not go any farther.

"Near the Long Stone?" Charlie was horrified. "Oh, really, Jasmine, it's about two miles away. How could you leave her?"

It was not until she had gone tearing back to Stephanie that the full import struck her. Jasmine had been vague about the Long Stone, she was not one for folklore or even for maps, but the general area was green and open and quite lonely.

"It's frightful, but what did I tell you?" was Stephanie's comment. "That's the sort of thing Jasmine does. I couldn't bear Ken to marry her," she added startlingly. "You think he's in love with her. I hope not."

"I wonder what she would think if I answered her truthfully," Charlie thought. It took some strength not to reveal the passion with which her heart rejected the thought of Kenneth's marrying anyone.

"Could I borrow your car?" she asked diffidently.

"By all means," Stephanie returned. "I'll mind the menagerie and keep an eye out for Ken." She laughed as Nicky pressed obstinately against his mistress's legs. "Oh well, perhaps you'd better take him."

A minute later Charlie was bumping over the cattle grid and heading for Hopehampton. She looked along the road for Samantha with optimism rather than judgment. The child could hardly have got this far. She hesitated at the fork by Well Hill, plumped for the right-hand arm and went down.

It was tiresome of Jasmine. Lunch would be ruined and so would Samantha's new dress. It had been so pretty, it made one's blood boil to think of it being trailed over fields and along dusty roads.

Charlie looked crossly ahead as she passed Friday Street. Still no sign. She drove on, losing the quaint stone houses first on one side and then on the other. Green fields with here and there a hay barn were now the order of the day. She followed a left fork and looking across saw the Long Stone in the distance.

A man passed and she let down the window and asked if he had noticed a little girl in a long dress. He had not. She used the footpath to reverse in and branched away from the Long Stone. It was hopeless and scarifying. If she found it so difficult to find the way how on earth would Samantha cope—although presumably she had known where she wanted to go.

Charlie was driving in circles and the place seemed singularly devoid of people. There weren't even animals in the fields. It was still and open and old, just as the way to the Devil's Churchyard had felt that Sunday. 'I don't think we can be far from there,' she decided. 'I've probably hit the road at some different point.'

It was not her favourite place. She would be glad to find Samantha and get safely home. It was very fanciful, she knew, but who could be sure that the feeling of anxiety she had experienced here two weeks ago had not been the shadow cast by the very real anxiety she was feeling now. If a place gave off the odour of its past, why not its future?

Nicky, at that moment, sat up and barked. Dogs, of course, were psychic creatures. "Now have you seen something?" Charlie asked him. "And is it something that I can see too?"

The next few seconds answered her. He had indeed seen something, not Samantha, alas, but another dog. It was old and scruffy and familiar. Behind it plodded the raggedy figure of Martha. The old woman would be no help since she could not speak, and yet it was worth a try.

Charlie stopped and leaned her head through the window. "I'm looking for Samantha," she said clearly. "Have you seen her?"

As anticipated, the response was nil, but some flicker in the battered leathery features spurred her on. This time she got out and held the old vagrant by the sleeve. "Martha, I'm very worried. If you know please help me. Have you seen Samantha today?"

Still there was silence.

"Look at me, Martha," Charlie commanded. "If you have, nod your head."

It worked. The man's tweed cap which Martha wore perpetually moved up and down.

"Oh, if only you could speak!" Charlie said impatiently. "Kenneth and Sam understand you, why can't I?" All she had was sign language. She used it as best she could. Martha stared, her eyes peering like raisins.

"Oh, what's the use?" Charlie gestured despairingly and turned to get back in the car. For sheer annoyance Nicky was unsurpassed. He chose that moment to spring out of the car and exchange sniffs with the tousled old mongrel at Martha's side.

"Oh, come on, Nicky," Charlie said forcibly. "Heel!"

" 'T'won't matter," Martha remarked casually. "He'll not harm 'im."

Charlie jumped. She even looked up at the sky to see where the voice was coming from.

"Taken to each other, they have," Martha said with satisfaction. She enjoyed the sight for a second and then looked away. "She'll be up there, I reckon. Leastways, that were the plan. Once I told 'er, she wanted one for you. 'Tes a ruin now, you see, all to pieces, the old Park. You'll not be able to bring the car up. But there she be, the old Park, right in the middle of nowhere. You look for 'er there." The speech had been an effort. She pointed up the road, swung her arm about and shuffled off.

All to pieces, the old Park, Martha had said. Charlie drove slowly looking from right to left because that last arm swing could have meant anything. About half a mile from the spot where she had met the old woman was a broken-down gate and far on the horizon the sorrowful pile of an empty house. *Right in the middle of nowhere.*

"You can say that again," Charlie conceded as she braked.

So Samantha was up there, was she? Engaged in what ploy? If nature had taken over what would be there? Dog roses were a possibility. She remembered the Sunday Kenneth had asked her to tea and Samantha's valiant flower arrangements. She was a romantic child. It would be like her to have a wild garden and to keep it secret.

But she *had* wanted to give some of it away. To me, Charlie recalled. It was a touching thought, but then Kenneth's daughter had always been touching—and very dear. "I must try not to spoil the secret," Charlie resolved as she locked the car. Nicky had leapt out, determined not to be left behind. She grabbed his lead and started up the field.

Rescuing Samantha was becoming quite a habit.

Who owned 'Old Park'? It was plain that nobody lived in it. Its roof was stripped in places and some of the window glass smashed. She saw no flowers that might have attracted Samantha. In fact she saw nothing or nobody.

"Samantha, are you there?" she called. "It's Charlie, Sam. Can you hear me?"

There was no answer.

Could the child have got inside the house and fallen? The thought was quelling but unlikely. Someone had boarded up the front door with sheets of metal. Charlie shrugged her shoulders and went round to the back. There must at one time have been a fire. Tinkers, she hazarded, or squatters. The wall was blackened and the back door stood ajar.

"It's not hide and seek, Sam," Charlie called sharply. "If you're there say so!"

She gathered Nicky's lead and went into the kitchen. It smelled of damp and was empty. The hall was dark. No light could filter through the metal sheeting on the front door. She was pretty sure Samantha could not be in the house, but obviously she had to search. All the room doors into the hall were shut. She found one locked and tried the next. It opened with a creak.

She found herself looking down the barrel of a gun.

The gun was in the hand of a young man with long dark hair. Sitting on the floor behind him was Samantha.

"Charlie!" the child shrieked, and made to get up.

"I told you, keep your trap shut," the youth commanded. He swung round threateningly.

Charlie noted that his hand was shaking. Was there a chance—if one played it cool?

"We've been looking for her everywhere," she said

sternly. "I don't know what her father is going to say to her. Come on, Sam. You're a very naughty girl."

It didn't work. The young man's right hand continued to hold the gun, His left one dragged her into the room.

"Sit down or you know what you'll get," he muttered.

Charlie did so with dignity. She felt extraordinarily undismayed. Perhaps it was his youth and the fact that he so obviously had the jitters. Perhaps it was the priority of Samantha, who must at all costs be reassured.

"I don't like dogs," the young man eyed Nicky balefully. "Can't have the dog." He pointed the gun.

Charlie's heart went cold. "Don't play round with that thing. It might go off."

"I kill dogs. Killed one this morning," their captor boasted. "If he squeaks he's for it."

He looked from Charlie to Samantha and back again to Charlie. There seemed little doubt that he was the Peeping Tom about whom Kenneth had warned her. Not too alarming, she told herself bracingly. She certainly did not believe that he had killed a dog that morning. From the way his hand was shaking he would never have the nerve to fire that gun, and for all she knew it need not even be a real one.

All she had to do was keep calm and when the opportunity presented itself slip out the back door. She thought hopefully that they might even do so at that moment, for the man had gone outside—only, alas, to stand in the hall. She supposed the word was 'cover'. He was 'covering' the door through which they would have to go.

"Don't be frightened," she whispered to Sam. "He won't do us any harm, but we may have to get away one by one." Once again Sam was showing that she was her father's daughter. She was as white as a ghost but dry-eyed. "I don't want him to hear us talking," Charlie went on, "so don't say anything. Just listen and nod your head. I'm going to distract his attention, at the moment I'm not sure how. When I do, you must slip out the back door. *Without waiting for me.* That's very important. Do you understand?" The head nodded, the new bell-shaped hairstyle swinging prettily. "Once you're out, run for all you're worth. Go to the first house and tell them. Ask them to phone the police. And tuck your dress into your pants. It doesn't matter what you look like. You have to run." Hard to know how far she should go. Samantha had a key role to play, but she was only in her eighth year.

"What will you do, Charlie?" the child was now whispering.

"I'll follow. I want you to go first. Are you brave enough?"

Again the head nodded.

"Good, that's settled, then," Charlie said briskly. "When the chance comes—run. Don't wait for me."

It was strange to think that less than two hours ago her mind had been occupied by the triviality of going out to lunch in the casual clothes she had put on for a 'mooching' day at home. She felt a bit silly as she straightened her belt and smoothed the blue sleeves of her shirt. The youth was still in the hall.

"What's upstairs?" she asked him. "Will you show me?"

He swung round, waving the gun. "I told you, keep down!"

If he likes—looking at people, Charlie thought, swallowing a gulp, he might as well look at me. She met the crazed eyes steadily with her own. Kenneth had once said the blue shirt made them look bluer still. "I'm not bad-looking," she thought. "Can I make him concentrate on me for five minutes?"

"Hello," she said. It sounded ridiculous.

He neither moved nor spoke, but at least the gun was no longer waving about.

"Do you know what this place is?" Charlie asked. "I believe they call it Old Park. Is that right?" She waited and as there was no response spoke again. "I'm not going to fight you. And it isn't a trap or anything. I'm all by myself. If you'd put that thing away we could talk. Why not?"

The young man hesitated. She thought he must hear her heart beating. His forehead beaded. Suddenly he grabbed her hand.

The time margin was razor-thin. She could not risk a backward look to check that Samantha had taken her chance. The stairs were worn and on the landing all the doors were open. Essential to keep from the window where Samantha, she hoped, would be visible running down the field. Charlie uttered words that were stupid, phrases that were quite meaningless.

"Dear God, don't let him touch me," she prayed. "Dear God, let Sam get away."

And then he did touch her, not so much amorously as roughly. His hand was hot and strong, pinching into her arm. She cried out and Nicky came bounding upstairs and into the room.

She thought the young man's fuddled brain had forgotten Nicky. Now he looked dark and menacing. She was afraid for the dog. You never knew.

"Nicky, go away!" she said sharply.

He barked, running between her and the youth. Poor Nicky. No expertise. Plenty of spunk.

"Go away!" she said again.

Kenneth had once said Nicky would be no protector. But he had given his heart. She was his. She had cried out. He would not budge.

The youth made a crooked gesture with the gun. It went off. Nicky keeled over and lay still.

Charlie saw it unbelievingly. It had been so quick, so casual, like stamping on an insect. For a few seconds she looked, deafened and still dazed, at Nicky's body. Then everything seemed to explode. He had killed Nicky. Nicky who had only wanted to protect her. Nicky who had loved her *and waved at her*.

The last memory was too much. Charlie felt her fingers dig into the long dark hair. She pulled and scrabbled, wriggling and twisting. She wanted to hurt. At that moment even Samantha faded from the plan of action. She fought blind and raggedly. She could not have hoped to win.

When she saw his arm go up with the gun in it, she was still too demented to care. And when the pain came, roaring through her head, she never doubted that she had been shot. He stood looking at her with a sick twist to his mouth. It brought a hairsbreadth of clarity. She was on her feet, she could still move. He was deranged and slow. Self-preservation was an instinct. She obeyed it, stumbling across the room.

She got to the corridor before he followed. Something was trickling warmly down the back of her neck. She made for one of the other rooms, hoping to elude him, and heard him shout out behind her in a sort of animal fear. The room was not empty. She saw shapes, rearing hooves, the curve of horns, and glimmering white faces. They were not human.

She was gaping at them when he reached her. He was gibbering with fear but dogged. The gun was still in his grip and he felled her with one blow.

Charlie thought the unicorns were dancing. Yet again they had come to the rescue of a girl in peril and now they were rejoicing. It was like being in the middle of Jean's picture.

Kenneth was there. He held out his arms and they danced together. His hair edged darkly on his tanned cheek. His smile was sweet and gay.

Charlie had that saddest of all feelings that she would have to wake up, and presently her eyes stirred tiredly. She closed them again, but it was only grey. No unicorns, no music, no Kenneth.

As the fog cleared she felt warmth against her leg. It was heavy and solid and it pressed. Her head throbbed as she raised it and for a moment she thought she was still dreaming or in the limbo of unconsciousness. Snuggling close to her was a white kid, across the floor was another. The room was full of goats. A great white billy stared back at her, his beard motionless.

Now everything came flooding back—the youth who had held her hostage, the struggle and the fantasy of the unicorns. Obviously the goats had discovered the old house and used the upper floor of it as a shelter. She had no doubt that they had saved her from being dispatched more effectively. They had looked unearthly, she could vouch for that. He had plainly thought them visitors from the supernatural.

"I must get up," Charlie thought. It was disconcerting that she could not. Her weakness was appalling and there was a sticky mess on the back of her head.

The gladness at being alive began to ebb. She thought

of Nicky and the tears rolled down her face. She remembered Samantha reading the lesson and the chill it had produced. '*My son, God will provide himself a lamb.*' All of it had come true.

Weakness made the time drift rather than tick. She could not move and the kid stayed where it was. A scrabbling sound outside did not disturb it. Charlie prepared herself, not knowing for what. Her heart turned over as she saw framed in the broken window glass two pricked-up sable ears. In the next instant Max's face looked in at her. It dropped out of sight, sinking her hopes, but only, as she realised, to gain purchase for the leap.

Lightly and accurately, Kenneth's beautiful dog sprang through the aperture. He loped to the spot where she lay and licked her face. When she put her arms limply about his neck he stayed consolingly for a second and then was away.

Minutes later he was back and behind him brown hands eased up the broken window and Kenneth's head and shoulders came through. She was to learn later that her captor was downstairs guarding the back door but that the room into which she had blundered was in a return with a sloping roof below it. She was to hear how Max had sniffed her out and how Kenneth had sent him up to reconnoitre and had then followed himself.

All that registered at that moment was Kenneth staring down at her as though he could not speak and then folding her, still wordlessly, with his arms.

CHAPTER THIRTEEN

CHARLIE was four days in hospital. The injury to her head was no more than a scalp wound and it healed well. Information was fed to her by her mother, whom she had never seen so subdued.

The young man, a former mental patient, was now in safe custody. The police had taken him away, quite unresistingly. And Kenneth? Oh, they weren't pleased with Kenneth, Ruth had said solemnly. They did not like civilians putting themselves at risk. They had arrived to find Kenneth and the youth discussing football coupons, the youth had been smoking a cigarette, the gun was in Kenneth's hand. Upstairs, Max had been guarding Charlie. That was not news. Through the mists, Charlie had sensed that she was not alone. Now and again a kindly tongue had touched her.

About Nicky Ruth would not talk. "Try not to think about it, baby. I promised Sister you wouldn't get upset."

For the first forty-eight hours Charlie was allowed no visitors except her mother. Ruth was being put up at the Dower House and each day she brought in something from Woodsgift; raspberries from Stephanie, a small yellow-fleshed melon grown in Jean's greenhouse and a bunch of roses with a card *'Con amore*, Ken, Sam and Jay'. It meant 'with love'. In any language a conventional message. She had to drum that into her stupid head because the first thing she had thought of was : "It's in Italian. I wonder was he thinking of the night we talked about 'collecting' Italy."

On her third day in hospital the 'no visitors' edict was relaxed. Jean, who had driven Ruth over, paid a five-minute call, Guy, who had already seen her *ex officio*, stayed longer and, in the afternoon, a sudden rather timid knock came to the door. Charlie called : "Come in," and Samantha's flushed face appeared. She was not alone. Charlie stared idiotically at the big broad-shouldered figure now closing the door.

"How are you?" he asked gently, taking her hand. "We won't stay long, I promise. We just wanted to have a look at you."

When you thought too much about a meeting it was never what you expected. What had come over Kenneth to make him seem as though he were walking on tiptoe? When excitement sent Samantha's voice up a semi-tone he was instant in frowning her down. At the end of ten minutes he looked pointedly at his watch and then at his daughter. "Haven't you got something to say before we go?"

"I'm very sorry," Samantha began hesitantly. "It was all a mistake. When I got there they were only rotten old goats."

"My client means," Kenneth put in, "that acting on information received, she expected to find a unicorn bank."

"I told Martha what I wanted," Samantha went on crossly. "I described it to her. She said there was one there."

"It looked very like it on Sunday," Kenneth said quietly. "Right size, right colour, just one horn away. When I found you—" his eyes met Charlie's, "I thought the tile had come true."

Charlie was taking in that Samantha had wanted to give her a unicorn and had asked Martha's opinion on where to start. There had been a certain lack of communication, but the old woman had done her best. She had known about the little herd of goats in the deserted house and the rest was history. All that remained to be told was that Samantha had made her escape as instructed, but the nearest house was a good distance away and she had been standing on the doorstep trying to persuade the elderly inhabitant that it was not a joke and the police should be telephoned when Kenneth had come along in the estate car with Max. On returning from Marshall's End he had heard from Stephanie as much as she knew and had set out immediately to join the search.

"I don't know what one says on an occasion like this," he commented quietly. "Except that I won't forget it or your total disregard of self. My family and I owe you more than I can ever repay.

She had known he would be grateful and ungrudging in his thanks. He was that kind of man. He had put it all quite beautifully and she would have given the world for one dry old-style reproof. Perhaps things would change after the weekend when she got back to work. Disappointment yet again. That was not to be contemplated, Kenneth informed her. After two cracks on the head with a gun barrel she had been extremely fortunate to escape serious injury, but the doctor had decreed at least a fortnight's rest.

When she left hospital, it was to go to Stephanie's house. There had been more than one choice. Her mother wanted to take leave and look after her at home. Jean Wychwood had been equally pressing for her to go to the Dower House, but Stephanie's invitation had won the day. It was Woodsgift without the slight awkwardness of being under Guy's roof and Stephanie had a flair for being welcoming without being fussy.

Kind as she was, she could be a dragon when she thought Samantha and Jason were encroaching on her guest. Charlie got up late and went to bed early; sunbathed in a chair on the terrace and, after a few days, progressed to taking Bobby for walks. He was a well-behaved dog, trotting along decorously on short legs. He did not gambol or twist his lead round her and he did not utter joyful 'wow-wow' barks. The one who had done these things had paid the price of his brief happiness. Charlie hoped Stephanie did not guess how difficult it was at times to play with another dog.

"What happened—to Nicky?" she had forced herself to ask.

"I took him," Kenneth answered gravely.

It was like him to have respected even the body of a little dog.

Three days passed peacefully. The children were indignant with Stephanie, who told them it was the wrong time of year to put food on the bird table because worms were plentiful and provided better nutriment.

Samantha came in to cut the hedge and to talk. "I wonder if Jasmine will ever come back. I don't care whether she does or not. She was beastly on Sunday. All the way out she kept tearing me off a strip."

"Well, she was in a hurry," Charlie deprecated. "Of course she'll come back."

"She mightn't—I heard Daddy say so. She's with a friend in London. It might be a long time before she gets tired of him."

"Oh, Sam, please don't!" Charlie reproved. This was appalling for Kenneth. If his world had crashed so drastically it was no wonder he seemed so quiet and was so little in evidence.

"Oh, I think he's got a patient on his mind," Stephanie volunteered. "Something quite tricky. I know he's been spending hours at the surgery. The first operation wasn't a success."

"Oh dear, I should be helping him," Charlie fretted. "Why won't he let me? I'm perfectly fit."

That evening she watched for the blue estate car to come home and waylaid its driver at the garage door.

"All right, come in. What's the trouble?" Kenneth enquired. "Emergency?" His face changed and grew determinedly casual. "Quite true, Charles. You must be psychic." A pet rabbit had been brought in by a distraught small boy who vowed it had eaten putty and would it die?

At least his eyes were twinkling and at least he had called her Charles. It nerved her. "I wanted to say I was sorry—about Jasmine."

"Oh yes?" he encouraged. "I thought you might be. She's shacked up, as they say, with Don."

"I don't give a fig about Don," Charlie said vehemently. "At least not in that sense. I was thinking about . . ."

"Me?" he interposed smoothly. "Is that it, Charles? Are my hopes supposed to be blighted? Tell me."

If only he did not sound so sarcastic. She realised the situation was delicate, but to see him as he had been since Sunday, so deflated and unlike himself, had been heart-breaking. "I'd never have put it like that, Ken. I don't think there's a person living could blight you," she thrust out of sheer hurt. "But yes, I did get the impression you cared for Jasmine and were only waiting for her to accept living in the country."

"Presumably you got the impression from Jasmine?" He was, she sensed, quite angry. "Then, my dear Charles," he went on as she nodded diffidently, "I suggest you revise your impressions. A halfway house such as you describe would be no use to me. Should the time ever come for me to ask someone to marry me the only answer I'd take would be yes or no. Mind you," he added casually, "I don't say I haven't thought about it, but Jasmine was never on the list."

"But—you always seemed so friendly . . ."

"I don't know whether you've noticed," he remarked, "but I'm friendly with many people. When it comes to love I'm probably not friendly at all. That's why I understand the unicorn. He smells pain and takes avoiding action."

Yes, that was the natural pattern for a man who had suffered. She acknowledged it silently. "I somehow can't imagine you in retreat," she said awkwardly. "Not of course that in my case there would be the necessity."

"No, Charles, I never feared you," he answered solemnly. "Not even when I thought you were going to be the curate's wife. Odd, isn't it, the way impressions get around?" There was another silence. He stood looking at her and shaking his head. "There must be no more of it, Charles, is that clear? Jasmine needs roots. She knows it and so do I. There's nothing I can do about it. Please contradict any rumours you hear to the contrary."

"You're not angry?" Charlie hazarded. "I only mentioned Jasmine because you seemed so—different."

"Different?" His brows knit. "In what way different?"

"Very nice," she said miserably, making it worse.

"I wonder what point I'm supposed to take from that?" he asked lightly. "Well, no matter. I'm getting a signal from Steph. It must be your supper time. Off you go, Charles. We'll finish this interesting discussion tomorrow when in any case we have got to talk."

"Why in any case?" she faltered.

"Because it's the last day of our month's trial. We have, I think, a mutual question to answer."

The easing of tension look was familiar. Charlie had seen it when Miss Roberts's cat had started to mend and after the operation on the vixen. If in past days Kenneth had had a patient on the danger list she judged that whoever it was had now recovered.

Stephanie had made a cheese pudding for supper. It was excellent, light and fluffy and in no way to blame for the fact that that night Charlie slept fitfully. An owl hooted persistently over the glen and she wondered if, across in his fork of the drive, Kenneth was also awake and hearing it.

Words spun in her head. '*He doesn't love Jasmine, not ever, not ever.*' They made a sort of carol to which a heart could dance. Of course he would marry eventually, tonight he had as good as said so—in the tone which she often felt was special to her because he thought her a nitwit—but it would not be Jasmine, who had never been good enough for him. "I'm like Stephanie, I couldn't have borne him to marry her," Charlie confessed, thumping the orange pillow. "But it's not my business. He may not even be going to keep me on."

It was a cold thought, slithering about her stomach, making her feel as though she were on a channel steamer during a bad crossing. So much had gone wrong in the month that would end tomorrow. 'I'll turn you into an asset if it kills me,' Kenneth had said.

Last Sunday four lives could have been lost instead of just one. Who could blame him if he took no more chances?

Outside in the dark the owl hooted and the sound was followed by squeaks. It was the sad part of living in the country and it seemed horribly attuned to her thoughts. Nothing went on for ever. She must be prepared to go.

In the morning Stephanie went to church and took the children with her. She had not said she was going to do this and Charlie, looking out from her bedroom window, had been surprised to see them run across hand in hand and get into the car. Kenneth's garage was open and empty and she had assumed he had taken them. Guy, she knew, had already left with Jean.

It left Charlie, apart of course from Max and Bobby, the only person in the glen. Not that she minded. It just made her feel a bit superfluous. Never mind, she would wash the breakfast things for a start and then get the vegetables ready for lunch. Perhaps cut off the 'deads' in her hostess's flower border. Stephanie had been bemoaning them the previous night.

Charlie put her breakfast tray on the dressing-table and set about making her bed. She saw the tail of a squirrel in the cupressus trees by Stephanie's car port and as she watched it ran along a branch. A few minutes later Bobby set up a shrill bark. She took it to be at the squirrel and did not look out. Unexpectedly Max's deeper rumble joined in. The two dogs seemed to be answering each other.

Bobby was not permitted to disturb the neighbours, but as no one was home today except herself Charlie felt disposed to be lenient. She had the breakfast things in the sink when the barking redoubled, from both sides. Astonishingly the noble Max was leaping like a puppy. Bobby, behind his barricade, was threatening to tear the place down.

"Quiet!" Charlie called, and stopped. Her heart had turned over. A week today and she was still hearing it, that phantom 'wow-wow' bark. Plainest of all this morning. Could there be truth in the fantasy that the spirits of animals returned to the places they loved? And that their friends recognised them?

She looked out and for the moment saw him, a short white dog with sad eyes and a merry tail. She knew it was an image because he was standing still. The real-life Nicky had never done that when chums were around.

The vision would be gone by the time she got outside, but she had to go because Bobby's frantic leaps might well pull down the wire.

The ghost dog did not fade. Nor did it move.

"I'm seeing it, like the unicorns," Charlie thought. Her eye lit stupidly on the left hind leg. *It was in a cast.*

At the same time Kenneth's voice said: "Snap!"

He had been standing out of sight. "I'm afraid he can't get to you yet. Yesterday was the first time he managed to stand," he said gently.

Charlie felt like a Catherine wheel. One minute she was on her knees beside Nicky, cradling him, feeling him lick her face. The next Kenneth had come over and was kneeling down beside them. All those days and nights at the hospital had been for this. He had thought it kinder not to raise her hopes in case they would have to be dashed. But again he had cared and been skilful—and the two together worked miracles.

She never knew how it was that she turned from the trembling dog and tearfully kissed his cheek. Or how it was that a second miracle happened. Arms went round her, lips pressed on hers, they lifted and returned and stayed while Nicky whimpered below.

"My dear, will you marry me?" Kenneth asked simply.

It sounded real, it felt real, and the bronzed neck over the tan-coloured bush jacket looked real. But of course it couldn't be. Charlie hid her face against the dark brown shirt.

"This is the point where you always go away," she whispered.

"You might find that handy for the future," he surmised. "So why not give it a whirl?"

"Are you sure?" Charlie asked politely. "I seem to have brought you nothing but trouble."

"You brought me yourself," Kenneth said softly. "A mouse in size, perhaps, but a mouse with the heart of a lion. And whatever happened you always came up smiling. I used to watch for that smile, Charles. I knew it would come. It made the world a better place, and then, gradually, I realised what it was all about."

She remembered that he had once said a unicorn could not be expected to change his nature. "Would it be bad for me to realise too?" she asked humbly.

"I don't want to rub it in," he said solemnly. "Just once, perhaps. Then we need never refer to the matter again." The smile that followed the teasing look was beautiful. "The singer of Rupert Brooke's *Song*, if you know it, tells my life story as well as his own. He ran away from love, so did I. You were a different kettle of fish."

His voice became reminiscent and she knew that he was quoting:

> "'And so I never feared to see
>   You wander down the street,
> Or come across the fields to me

> *On ordinary feet.*
> *For what they'd never told me of,*
> *And what I never knew;*
> *It was that all the time, my love,*
> *Love would be merely you.'* "

"Well, Charles?" he asked quietly, his eyes never more blue. He took her hands and held them in his own. "Let's go back to the beginning. Will you do me the honour of becoming my wife?"

A graceful question deserved a graceful answer. Charlie looked down at their linked hands and up at the face she loved.

She said demurely: "Your kind invitation is accepted with great pleasure."